MW01534726

MAIN MENU

CHAPTER 1

Atlanta, Georgia 2012

PATIENCE

The sounds of Future and Rihanna's latest hit blasted from Patience's factory speakers as she speed through downtown Atlanta for her first destination of the day.

She turned onto Courtland Street, entered the student parking lot, and was reluctant about going to class.

"Lord, please give me the strength to make it through another day's journey in this thing called life."

Patience uttered a silent prayer while continuing to stare blankly into space. Eventually, she pulled out her Mac lip-gloss and applied an even amount to her plump lips.

Patience was in her last year of graduate school. She often felt awkward studying counseling because most of the time, she felt lost with no concrete answers of her own. Patience had come a very long way from where she imagined; a very long way from where everyone else thought she would be as well. She had a plan that she was determined to accomplish, and she vowed never to let anyone or anything get in her way.

Patience spent the first eighteen years of her life being tossed from foster home to foster home. Growing up, she'd endured plenty and had countless reminders of the dark past she longed to forget. Patience tried her hardest to live by the saying "Never judge a book by its cover"; It was one of her favorite references used during her mock counseling sessions. All of her life people looked on as spectators; in awe as if it was some great movie or best-selling novel.

Kids were jealous of her; however, she had no idea why anyone would want to be in her shoes. She was a foster kid with no family. Everyday life for her was no walk in the park, but people never even considered her struggles or hardships. She learned that her beauty was appealing, and people judged a person's looks instead of getting to know the actual story behind it all. Time and experience taught her that sometimes people saw things in her that she didn't see. People saw her greatness and significance without her even making a sound, and that fact alone made her even more ready to start her life's dream of becoming a counselor.

Patience was known for her light brown eyes that normally lit up any room she entered. Her small nose and shapely plump lips that held a beauty mark slightly above gave her a childlike appearance. She was absolutely breathtaking, which she had heard quite often, but she never used her looks as a means of living. Her looks didn't make a promising past for her, so she surely wasn't going to rely on it for her future.

Patience hopped out of her 2012 Dodge Charger and adjusted the waist of her Seven jeans while pulling her gray blazer over her shoulders. She popped the trunk and proceeded to rummage through all of the many items her trunk possessed, in search for a scarf, anything to compete with the crazy December winds that were blowing so hard. When she found a scarf, she hastily threw it around her neck and walked the normal mile and a half to get to her only of the day.

Before Patience could enter class and get prepared for her normal hour lecture from her professor, Ms. Strangler walked in and asked to speak with her. She plastered a fake smile on her face to cover her aggravation, grabbed her Macbook and her large Michael Kors handbag, and hit the door heading to the student center, a place she dreaded.

Before she could take a seat or get comfortable with her surroundings Ms. Strangler started, "Patience darling, you know that in order to maintain your scholarship you must start some sort of volunteering efforts."

Patience stared at Ms. Strangler for a moment before she spoke.

"I've been a student here for four years already. If I didn't understand I don't think I'd still be here, don't you agree?" Patience mockingly stated to the white lady sitting in front of her.

Ms. Strangler reached down to open a compartment on her desk and pulled out a manila folder, obviously ignoring Patience's comment. She politely reached her long arm across the desk, revealing a diamond-encrusted bracelet while handing her the folder.

Patience swiftly snatched the folder from Ms. Strangler and pulled out the contents, which looked to be a plane ticket, card key, and a short and simple note.

Ms. Patience Smith,

We need you to attend a number of conferences, beginning this Saturday. In the envelope, you will find your round trip plane ticket to New York and the key card to the hotel that you will be staying in. Sorry for the late notice, it's only one little weekend away from home. Remember we are trying to help you successfully complete your degree by utilizing your scholarship. Look at it as a trip away from home and 200 hours towards your

volunteer scholarship. We will provide you with
further details on the next two conferences.

　Thanks,
　Scholarship Team

　When Patience finished reading the note, she saw a slight smirk on Ms. Strangler's face. She figured she had no choice but to oblige or get kicked out of school so she grabbed her belongings and headed back to class.

　When she arrived, there was a note on the door from her professor stating that class had been dismissed early, along with homework for the week. Patience pulled out her iPhone and began typing the details into her calendar as she prepared for the cold walk back to her car.

　Patience, being a ward of the state for most of her life was offered the luxury of attending any college of choice once graduating high school on the states expense. Patience decided to stay in the only state that she was familiar with after graduating from Frederick Douglass High School, so she attended Georgia State University.

The terms of her free education meant that she had to volunteer a certain numbers of hours doing something related to her field. During her undergrad, she volunteered at Grady Hospital and worked along with psychologist who worked with the mental disabled. She found that to be very beneficial to her resume and physical experience. Unfortunately, she couldn't continue volunteering after she completed undergrad, so she stopped her volunteer efforts all together.

Patience spent months avoiding the volunteer team after attending her first conference at the W hotel downtown a few months ago. However, they finally caught up with her. She hated the fact that they basically controlled her life with the many conferences that they demanded she attend. Spending long hours listening to the plans and development efforts of different Counseling Agencies was not her found passion.

As Patience jumped in the car and slammed the door, she contemplated on going home, or to the club. Since her day was cut short, she decided she would head to the club and tell her boss that she wasn't going to be available next weekend.

During the short ride to the club where she worked as a dancer, all she could think about was her money being cut short. This would really interfere with her plans, but not attending the conference was out of the question.

Patience pulled up to Magic and threw her school gear in the trunk, while retrieving her work gear. She tossed the large PINK bag over her shoulders and proceeded into the building. Once inside she spotted the person she needed to see, and continued to his office in the back of the club.

King was the owner of the club and damn near every strip club in Atlanta. King was a ruthless dude; blunt and straight to the point was his motto. He was cool with Patience though; she was best friends with his main lady Jade and she made him thousands of dollars on a daily basis.

She worked at the club three nights a week while dedicating the other nights to her studies. Patience was very headstrong and was a lady that moved by her rules only. She was not the average stripper. When she was working, Patience just danced. She did not carry on conversations with the customers or other dancers. Many of the patrons were very interested in Patience due to her mysterious nature, which was even better for her pockets.

Patience did her secret knock on King's door while leaning her tired body on the wall and announced, "It's me, P!"

Trick, King's three hundred pound friend and bodyguard, appeared at the door and let Patience enter.

"Take a seat P. what's up? Is everything sweet?" King asked while finishing f his blunt and dumping the bud into the ashtray beside him.

King's office was very large and was fit for a King. King sat in a large chair that had real gold implanted around the edges. His walls were red and black with the word *King* drawn on the surrounding walls. Self-portraits covered other parts of the wall.

Patience tossed her bag on the floor beside her, and took the scarf from around her neck revealing the tattoo on her chest that spelled out the word "blessed" in big bold Mongolian letters. Patience removed her blazer and put King up to speed on her future business with his establishment. She knew this would be hard, breaking the news to him that she would have to cut her days down to once a week after this week, but all in all, she knew he would understand.

When Patience was done, King spoke.

"I know you have a plan, but you one of my best girl's, P. You make the most money in this bitch and you only in here three days out the week. You don't do the private shows; you don't even take all your clothes off. Now you're telling me that you can only do one day?"

Patience stood up and positioned herself directly in King's face. "I explained the details to you in full, King. You're absolutely right; I do have plans, and they never consisted of working for you forever. You can either take my offer or leave it!"

Patience was praying that King agreed to her plans. She needed the one day at the club to provide for her daily necessities. She knew she would have to cut back on her weekly shopping trips to Phipps Plaza and her online shopping habits, but that wouldn't be too hard. She grew up with nothing so she could manage just fine.

Unfortunately, she knew what kind of man King was. King was an egotistical bastard that treated women like shit on the bottom of his shoe. He even treated her friend Jade like a child and not a woman. King did numbers to Jade's self esteem by constantly cheating on her and lashing all kinds of verbal slants at her, so why in the hell did she even think he would care about her.

After a long ten seconds of silence and King looking at Patience as if he wanted to slap the life out of her, he stood and simply said, "Done!"

Patience grabbed her bag, threw her blazer back on, and wrapped her scarf around her neck while holding King's gaze. She couldn't believe he wasn't being the selfish bastard that he normally was. She knew he didn't give a damn about her plans or her future; all he was concerned about was his money. So what was it that made him agree? She thought to herself, not knowing that she would soon find out.

"Thanks!" Patience muttered as she left the office, letting out a deep breath once making it to the other side of the door.

CHAPTER 2

We plan the way we want to live, but
only God makes us able to live it.

-Proverbs 16:9

REGGIE

"Tell me a little about yourself, Mrs. Rivers?
Why did you choose this line of work?" Reggie
asked his interviewee as he reclined in his leather
chair. He stared sternly waiting for a reply, before
glancing at the Breitling watch hanging from his
wrist to check the time.

"I've always had an interest in behavioral
healthcare. I have three years of experience working
as a therapist aide in a facility similar to this one,"
Mrs. Rivers nervously explained. "I've worked with
children and their families to create behavior plans
that fit the child's daily lifestyle. I enjoy making a

difference in the lives of others, and I look forward to working with you and your team."

Mrs. Rivers was quite shocked to know that the owner of the well-known Dupree Youth Behavioral Clinics held the appearance of a street thug. She looked at Mr. Reggie Dupree and noticed the many tattoos covering his hands; she was even more shocked to see them covering his mocha colored face. His dreads were braided back and pulled into a neat ponytail, which enhanced his beautiful features.

The only thing that led her to believe that she was in the right place was his extremely neat appearance. Reggie wore an Armani ash gray striped white and black button down shirt with matching black slacks. His shirt was stitched with the initials RD in the right hand corner pocket, and his demeanor spoke measures. Anyone that came in contact with him could tell that he was a humble man that possessed money, power, and respect. The mere fact that she had never seen him and he was talked about for his superb treatment facilities for youth around the States let her know that he was a very low-key type of guy.

Reggie gave Mrs. Rivers a once over and from just looking at this older lady he could tell that she had class. Reggie had dealt with his share of people in his twenty-eight years of living. Not always had he been this well renewed businessman known for providing a second chance to the youth. He had once been the man in the streets providing many families with grief on all ends.

"Ok, the job is yours. First, I need for you to bring this packet back in tomorrow fully completed. I also need for you to provide the company with your own federal and state background check and drug test by end of the week," Reggie instructed as he handed over the documents to his new employee.

"Thank you so much. This is dream come true."

Mrs. Rivers stood to shake his hand and accept the job packet. She displayed a big bright smile as she thanked Reggie for the opportunity of a lifetime. Reggie led her out and sighed, happy that his day of interviewing was finally over. He made a mental note to hire an assistant to help out with the hiring. Although he was a very selective guy when it came to his companies, he just couldn't handle eight offices here in Georgia all alone.

Mrs. Rivers had been his seventh candidate this week, and the best one yet, so he offered her the position. Reggie continued into his office, closed his door, and palmed his face with his full hands. He had everything any man could want; money, cars, fame, fortune, but he oftentimes felt that something was missing.

Reggie spent the rest of his workday contacting his other twelve offices ensuring that all plans and goals were submitted for the month, and putting his employees up to speed on the new treatments by giving one on one training sessions to avoid the dreadful staff meetings. In his last training session, he was hit with some news that he didn't care to hear.

"You have a line of Conferences planned for the future Mr. Dupree. I'll have everything you need tomorrow for your first one in New York this upcoming weekend."

Reggie's assistant stated as she handed Reggie a printout of the scheduled conferences.

Reggie really did enjoy his new lifestyle, it gave him a sense of peace and he didn't have to worry about always looking over his shoulders, but it was also annoying at times. Due to him being the owner of a chain of behavioral clinics for the youth, the federal government required yearly conferences to discuss the company's mission and plans for the future.

With there being many other companies just like his, he knew that he would have to attend at least three conferences before he would present his presentation. Lucky for him, he already had everything mapped out. Being the owner of his own chain of businesses had always been a dream for Reggie. He didn't want just any old business; he wanted something that would benefit his people instead of break his people down.

"Have that for me in the am, I'll be in at ten sharp," Reggie ordered to Stacy as he retrieved his Louis V briefcase from the shelf and exited the office heading towards his black on black 2012 BMW x6 Truck.

Reggie was tired, and a little vexed after his long workday. He knew the exact place to go for a quick drink; something to relax him just a little, but first he wanted to find out which spot his boy was at for the night.

"Aye, which spot you at?" Reggie yelled through the phone over the loud music blaring through the truck's speakers.

"I'm at Magic. Come on, I got us a section ready," King laughed, knowing that the entire spot belonged to him.

"Alright, be there in twenty have my bottle and my bitch ready," Reggie laughed half-heartedly as he turned on Peachtree Street en route to Magic, which was on the west side of town.

King was Reggie's right hand man when he ran in the streets years ago. They were still tight like two flat tires even though Reggie wasn't in the streets anymore. King owned five prestigious gentlemen clubs in Atlanta. Fantasy, Wish, Luck, Charm, & Magic housed some of the finest in the city. His clubs were the go-to spots for all of the hustlers, ballers, rappers, white-collar workers, and tourists here in Atlanta.

King was the total opposite of Reggie. He was loud, flashy, flamboyant, and downright disrespectful to any and everybody. Many people feared King, especially the girls who worked for him. King and Reggie's relationship lasted by the means of a seven-letter word *R.E.S.P.E.C.T.*

As Reggie pulled up to the club, he parked next to a candy apple red 2012 Dodge charger with the word *PATIENCE* engraved on the passenger door in Mongolian letters. Before he could hop out, the car sped out of the clubs entrance, leaving him wondering what woman would pull off before gracing him with attention.

Reggie was far from arrogant, however he knew his capabilities. He also knew the minds of the money hungry women in Atlanta that would do anything for a come up. Many knew him by his cars and his name rang bells around town. Normally when he would appear places women would do anything to get the infamous Regg's attention, but Miss Red Dodge was the least bit interested in him.

As soon as he entered the club, the many guests who frequented King's spots greeted him.

"What up Regg! My nigga, where the fuck you been man? You be missing on the scene, B," Trick slurred as he dapped Reggie up.

"Yea, a nigga try to keep a low profile out of respect for the hustle. Where the hoes at though? Ain't too much about me changed!"

Trick laughed and pointed around with his hands. "You mean to tell me, you don't see all this ass in the building? Go pick out one for the night, on the house!"

Reggie unbuttoned a few buttons on his Armani dress shirt and sat down on the plush circular sectional that held up the entire back wall of the club. "I'm just chilling for tonight. Go let King know I'm here."

"On it," Trick said as he headed to the back of the club. He was aware of his surroundings on the way, but did not notice Jade enter the club and go sit at the bar.

Loud music blasted throughout the club as naked females danced on stage and walked around pursuing their prey for the night. King had everything set out just as Regg expected with bottles of Patron and all types of food covering the tables.

"My motherfucking nigga Regg! Is that you, New Money?" King asked while walking towards Reggie. He was delighted to see his boy for the first time in months.

"It's me, nigga; in the flesh," Reggie dapped him up and gave him a brotherly hug.

The three men sat around the sectional and begin to pour drinks, while talking shit over the loud music and voices in the club. Reggie poured him another round and started to relax a little.

"So what's been going on out here in these streets? How's business?"

"What? Don't tell me New Money looking to join forces with me again, huh?" King gave off a hearty laugh. "Everything is everything, you know. I got my brother, Majesty, managing two of the spots. He bringing in major paper. I'm running the other three, and you can see how that's going for yourself."

"Yea, I see. You got me wondering if I'm in the right line of business." Reggie chuckled lightly while taking a shot back with no hesitations.

King noticed how his boy was throwing the drinks back so he asked him if he wanted any company from one of his ladies. Reggie assured him that he was just fine and they continued their reunion for another hour or so. They laughed so hard and drunk so much alcohol that Reggie was ready to call it a night and head home. He had to work early the next morning; not to mention packing for his short trip to New York for the conference.

Reggie stood as a tall, thick, sexy chick walked up and sat next to King whispering in his ear. Reggie shook King's and Trick's hands signaling his departure.

"Bruh, you out already? You too old to hang now?" slurred King as he stood to embrace Reggie with another brotherly hug.

"Yea, I'm out. It's shut eye time for me. Lots of money to be made my friends."

With that being said, Reggie walked out of the booth heading for the exit, as King and the thick stripper headed back for his office giggling and licking each other down in the middle of the crowd, not trying to be discreet at all.

Before Reggie got to the exit he noticed Jade leaving the bar and heading towards King's office with fury in her eyes that showed the deep hurt in her dark full round face. Reggie tried his best to distract her from heading in the direction of King and the stripper.

"Jade!" he yelled over the loud music.

Jade slowly turned her head and was relieved to see a familiar face. It was Reggie; Jade wondered why King wasn't like his friend, modest and gentle. Jade had known Reggie just as long as she'd known King, and she always respected him for treating her like a lady even when he was about that life. Reggie was not only King's friend, but also her best friend's big brother. Although he was rarely around when they were growing up due to his life in the streets, the few times she would spend the summers with Essence they would have their run-ins.

"Hey Regg," Jade somberly replied, giving him a hug and keeping her focus on the direction King was going.

"What you doing here girl? This ain't no place for a lady like you." Regg placed his arms on Jade's shoulder and walked toward the exit with her.

When they got out to the parking lot, Reggie walked with her to her brand spanking new silver 2013 Lexus G50.

"This you, Jade?" Reggie asked with a smirk on his face and his head tilted to the side.

"You can say that!" she stated while rubbing her finger on the shiny exterior of the car before taking a seat inside and cranking up the car. She pressed the seat warmer button to knock the cold air from her seats.

"I see you now! Get on to the house. King was just telling me he'd be heading there soon. Goodnight!" Reggie lied, while jogging to his truck trying to fight the cool November breeze.

Reggie had his share of saving his partners ass, and he thought that King was lucky that his girl was Jade and not any other chick because his ass would've been caught tonight. Reggie respected Jade enough to lie to her; hell, she was like a little sister to him. In his opinion, she was too good for King. But he was just another man, no one to judge. Reggie wasn't a saint, he just believed in respect. He lived by it, and expected others to as well.

Reggie pulled up to his condo in Atlantic Station and parked his truck inside of his garage. He wasn't too keen about his cars being in the parking garage so he opted to have a personal garage built on the side of his condo, where he kept all of his vehicles. Before getting out of the truck, he sat looking into the night sky, wondering just what was missing in his life.

CHAPTER 3

Trust in the Lord with all of your
heart and lean not on your own
understanding.

-Proverbs 3:5 21

JADE

Jade entered the club in her all black attire, trying not to stand out much in the crowd of partygoers. She didn't see the big deal in men wanting to give their hard-earned monies away to strippers; them doing so provided her with a roof over her head. If it weren't for the ballers and hard working men that frequently came to the clubs, she wouldn't be living the life that she lived.

Jade walked up to the bar and ordered a long island iced tea. She wasn't a heavy drinker but lately she'd been throwing back one too many. Hell, if it weren't for her best friends, Patience and Essence, she probably would have resorted to drugs.

Jade was the girlfriend of the notorious King, although she wasn't too proud to hold that title due to their years of on again off again love affairs. Lately, she'd been feeling like it held little to no meaning at all. She was slowly, but surely, becoming fed up with his ways.

Jade sat at the bar working on her fourth long island and going unnoticed by King's workers, and even King himself. Jade begin to sweat excessively so she shoved her long silky black hair into a high ponytail that fell down her back. She retrieved a napkin from the counter and dabbed at her face being sure not to wipe off her makeup that she just had professionally done before coming out to the club. She sat back and watched her man, until interrupted by Reggie.

Reggie decided to play the friend of the day for his low down and dirty buddy, so Jade played right along with him. Jade walked outside with Reggie while holding light conversation and pretended to leave the club. She parked her car across the street at the Towers liquor store and headed right back into the club once Reggie headed out in his BMW truck.

Making her grand entrance inside of the club, and going unnoticed for the second time in a row, she headed directly to his office and inserted the extra key King had provided for her.

When the door opened, she couldn't believe her eyes. In fact, she was stuck standing there in complete awe at the sight in front of her. With tears forming in her eyes, she mustered up enough strength to speak.

"So, this is how you do it now? First it was random hoes, now you're fucking your workers?"

King looked up as he heard a muffled voice coming from the direction of the door. Without even being apologetic, King pushed the dancer off his lap and flatly stated, "Everything's not what it seems. Why the fuck you coming up in here unannounced anyway? When you look for shit, it hits you right in your face. Are you satisfied now?"

Jade walked over to King and looked him directly in the eyes, pleading for him to at least say he was sorry, wanting him to explain this situation to her, needing him to just need her for a chance. As she continued to stare at him, she saw nothing. There were no signs that King even gave a damn that he was caught in this uncompromising position.

King had done his share in their relationship, but never had Jade caught him in the actual act. She definitely didn't expect him to have a nonchalant attitude about the situation. Even when Jade would find numbers in his pockets, or even see his sexual text messages with other females, he would always apologize and beg for her forgiveness. He would practically do anything to convince her that it was all a big misunderstanding.

Standing in his office today, with the sight before her eyes proved to her that she was becoming a pawn in his chess game. He no longer cared about her feelings; he disrespected her with no problem at all. She felt that all of the love was gone at this point. There would be no turning back.

As the stripper hurriedly placed her clothes back on, Jade was knocked back into reality.

She reached her hands towards King's face and rubbed at his smooth skin. She slowly moved her hands upward, massaging his curly locks in her hand.

"I loved you with my all, and I gave you all of me. I tried to be everything that you needed and more, but look at where it got me. Look at what you're doing to us. Why couldn't you just leave if you weren't happy with me, King?"

King pushed Jade's hand from his head and ordered Trick to remove her from his office. Jade fought back tears as she watched the man she loved react in such a harsh manner towards her.

"Let's go!" Trick spat, with a very distant look on his face, not giving Jade any eye contact but motioning with his hands for her to start moving.

As Jade and Trick walked through the club, she could hear the whispers and see the stares of the other dancers. She figured they were putting two and two together, and she felt like shit. She wondered if Patience knew about King's involvement with the other dancers, and just never told her. She wondered how long this had been going on right up under her nose. She had so many questions, when really none of it should have even mattered to her after being slapped right dab in the face with the truth.

When they finally reached her car, she jumped in and looked at Trick as the tears being to fall. Trick shook his head and headed back in the direction of the club without even uttering a word to her.

Jade sat in her car for half an hour and cried like a baby. Something in her hoped, no something in her prayed that King would run out after her and try to make everything right. Jade constantly peered out her rear view mirror and at her larger than life Samsung Galaxy tablet phone expecting King to at least call her, but he didn't. Jade was used to King's infidelity, but never to this extent. Jade was becoming someone else, in fact Jade was becoming like someone she once promised she would never turn out like.

"I love him," Jade cried out to no one in particular as she dried her tears away and looked out the window at the customers coming and going.

"This is what I deserve huh? I don't have the figure of a model and I could work on my weight a little, but why not just leave me instead of cheat?" Jade continued to cry out while looking at herself in the mirror under the sun visor.

Jade refused to go home that night and be anywhere near him, in fact she didn't know if she could ever be near him again. She quickly pulled out of the club's entrance and headed straight for downtown. When she arrived at her destination, she jumped out, handed her keys to the valet, and proceeded into the "W" hotel.

Jade walked into the hotel zoned out, in a zombie state to be exact as she headed directly to the desk to book her room for the night. The front desk seemed so far away from her and everything appeared to be so unbelievable.

"Baby, come here. What's the matter?" she heard a deep sexy voice say.

When she turned around, there was a sexy face to match that voice. She tried wiping the dried up tears from her eyes, but she was a little too late. He had already seen her at her worst.

"I'm fine. Please don't worry about me," she uttered, trying to keep her composer before breaking down in front of a complete stranger.

Jade turned to walk away from him and increased her pace as she resumed her path towards the reception desk. She was startled as he lightly grabbed at her arm before she could reach the desk. When she turned, she met his intense and caring gaze. That's when she noticed how handsome he was.

He stood 6'1 with the same type of glossy dark skin as her that glowed vibrantly. He was dressed in a gray True Religion jogging suit with smoky gray Timberland boots that brought out a rugged appeal in him. His curly black hair, which was set in a very low fade, brought out his large beautiful brown eyes. His eyes seemed to speak to her; his eyes were something she craved at that moment. She craved for someone to rescue her from the nightmare that she currently lived in.

"Come with me, please," he whispered as he grabbed her hand, sending chills through her entire body, and heading to the bar inside of the hotels lounge.

She was half-tipsy, hurt, and confused. She needed someone to talk to other than her girls. She knew that Patience would hear about all of the drama when she went in to dance Thursday night, and she didn't want to consume Essence with her relationship problems once again, so she figured that he was the perfect outlet for the night.

They sat at the bar for hours laughing and talking. She revealed to him the events of her night and she cried right in his arms. She felt so comfortable in his presence that she poured out everything about her and King's relationship. He listened intently and gave her sound advice and encouragement that replaced her once saddened frown with a smile.

They drank endless amounts of drinks, talked, laughed, and nibbled lightly on the shrimp and wings that they ordered. Jade had to admit to herself that after releasing everything from within, she felt like a brand new person. She knew that she had a long road ahead of her as far as healing was concerned, but Majesty provided her with the support that she desperately needed.

Majesty opened up to Jade as well, all throughout the night. He told her that he owned establishments in Atlanta and owned property and land back in Philly. Majesty enlightened Jade on a few events from his past relationships; he even told her a little about his daughter's mom who decided to pass over her rights and let him have custody at birth. He talked endlessly about his baby girl, Jewel; even showed Jade many pictures of his daughter that he kept in his wallet.

They were enjoying themselves so much that the time slipped by without them realizing it was the start of a brand new day. Jade realized that she never had the chance to book her a room, and she panicked, slowly snapping back into reality.

"It's pretty late, I'm going to go book a room now if…"

"I already have a suite booked so no worries. Besides, I want you with me for the night," Majesty confessed before Jade could complete her statement.

At this point they both were drunk and very comfortable around each other, but Jade was still reluctant about taking him up on his offer.

Jade looked at him with questionable eyes and stuttered, "I-I don't think that's a good idea. We don't know each other. I just met you."

Majesty looked into Jade's eyes, and she practically melted from their instant connection.

"True. Just trust me. Have I caused you any harm so far? I promise you I'mma take good care of you tonight."

Jade looked into his eyes one last time before smiling at him and following him to his suite on the thirteenth floor. Once inside the room, Majesty ran warm bath water for her as he undressed her. First, he removed her form fitting black bebe shirt and blazer. Then he removed her black bebe pants. Finally, he removed her lace-trimmed bra and panties and directed her towards the warm water. As her body adjusted to the hot water, he started with his orders.

"Lay your head back!"

Jade perched her lips preparing to speak, but he placed a finger to her lips and repeated his first order. As she laid her head back, he began washing her body with the lathering Dove body wash. He was so gentle with her, and she felt so safe with him, she released all of her fears and enjoyed the moment.

After fully washing her body down, he eased into the water behind hers. Jade became self-conscious as thoughts flooded her mind about King's disrespect towards her. King would call her every name in the book and throw her weight up in her face constantly, so remembering that she slowly tried to get out of the tub.

Majesty gripped her hips and sat her back down in front of him as he placed kisses all over her back, while whispering in her ear.

"You are beautiful. You are perfect, stunning, and sexy!"

Tears formed in Jade eyes. She wasn't used to this treatment. King had never made her feel loved like this. Here she was with a complete stranger that knew what she wanted. He knew what she needed without her even saying a word.

Majesty gently washed her face with a warm washcloth and then proceeded to place soft kisses all over her face.

At this point, Jade had all types of feelings and thoughts running through her mind.

What am I doing? This isn't right; it feels so right though. I don't even know him. I am losing it, losing my damn mind!"

After their bath, he laid her on the bed and dried every part of her body off, taking his time to remove all of the moisture. He rubbed her down with lotion and massaged her entire body until he heard soft moans escape her lips. He kissed her softly, entangling his tongue with hers, as they let their lips sing a song that felt so unfamiliar yet so recognizable to them both.

With no questions being asked about their pasts, and neither of them thinking about their futures, they laid there, bodies intertwined, holding on to each other for dear life as they fell asleep in each other's arms.

****

Jade was originally from Atlanta, but when her mother caught her father cheating she decided that packing up and leaving would make him stop. Philly was their third destination before her father finally decided to stop his cheating ways. It was also right before she experienced a life-altering event that still haunts her to this day.

Jade vowed to never be a weak woman like her mother; she vowed to never crave attention from a man to the point where she accepted anything from him. She grew to hate her mother weakness, which later turned out to be one of her own weaknesses.

Jade experienced a childhood that no child should have ever experienced. She watched the constant verbal and physical abuse that her mother endured. She sat up countless of nights consoling her mother, even praying with her mother hoping that she would finally leave her father. Jade had very few friends. Every time she grew close to someone, her mother would up and move due to her father's infidelity. This went on for most of her high school years until her father was struck with an illness and he had no choice but to stop.

Her father's stroke prevented him from getting around and he required her mother's full attention. To be honest, she thought that her mom was happy with his new physical condition; anything to be needed and to say that she was married was just fine with her. She didn't realize that she had a precious jewel watching her every move and would soon become just like her in so many ways.

Jade's mom became bored with constantly taking care of her father so she decided to live a little. She started doing the same exact thing her husband had done. His infidelity was the reason she moved her family from state to state, and now she was mimicking his actions and didn't feel bad about it at all. She became a new person; staying out late, sometimes not coming home at all, and leaving Jade to care for her dad.

While sitting in her last class of the day ready to get home and watch television she counted down until the bell would ring. When it rung, Jade sprinted out of class and jumped on her school bus. She looked out of the window at the beautiful sky and admired nature until she arrived at her stop. When she stuck her keys in the door to open it, she heard her mom.

"Please! Please, Jadel, don't do this! I am sorry! Sorry for messing up our family!"

"Shut up bitch, right damn now!" She heard her dad scream as he pistol-whipped his mom with a gun that she didn't even know existed.

She thought that her presence would calm the situation down so she cleared her throat. With tears in her eyes, she begged her dad to put down the gun.

"Come on dad; please just put the gun down. We can work this out."

For the first time ever, Jade saw her dad do something she never thought he could do; he cried. With tears flowing down his face, he walked to Jade and kissed her on the cheek.

"I'm sorry baby. I'm sorry for all of the pain I've caused you. Now it's time for me to take it all away."

Those were the last words Jade ever heard her father say before he shot her mother twice in the head and killed himself with one shot to the head.

She stood stone cold in the middle of the floor in total shock. She replayed the events in her mind as she watched both of her parents die right in front of her eyes.

$$****$$

That next morning Jade gazed around the room with a confused look on her face. Next to her on the small stand sat fresh strawberries, waffles, turkey bacon, and a glass of orange juice. She thought she was dreaming, and had a slight headache from her many drinks the night before. When she saw his face, that's when it all came back to her.

"Good Morning, beautiful!" Majesty walked towards Jade and kissed her cheeks when he noticed that she had awakened.

Jade rushed out of the bed and ran into the bathroom locking the door behind her. So many thoughts flooded her mind.

Did I have sex with a stranger? Why am I even here? What is going on?

Jade turned on the faucet and soaked her face with the ice-cold water. Jade was startled by a light knock at the door.

"Is everything alright, Jade?"

"Um…no, I mean yes. I will be out in a second."

Jade removed her hair from the tight ponytail and let it flow down her shoulders as it cascaded down her back. She sat on the bathroom floor resting her back against the door, fighting with her memory to reveal to her what happened last night. After sitting in the same spot for thirty long minutes, small bits and pieces came back to her.

She remembered his name was Majesty and she remembered how she poured her heart out to him. She recalled him being a complete gentlemen and a small smile crept across her face.

Jade peered over her shoulder and noticed a very large closet on the other side of the bathroom. Inside, her clothing was folded neatly and her shoes and other belongings next to them. Jade placed on all of her clothing, leaving her shoes and purse in place, and quietly departed from the bathroom. The first thing she noticed when she exited was Majesty's bright eyes staring at her intently. He stared at her as if he was reading her soul; as if he could read her every thought.

"Sorry for hiding out in the bathroom and I forgot to tell you good morning," Jade shyly acknowledged as she held her head up high trying not to let his intense stare intimidate her.

Majesty walked over to Jade and grabbed her hands while walking with her towards the bed. He sat down and patted the spot next to him, motioning for Jade to take a seat. Jade sat down. Before she could speak, he kissed her lips, and then placed by a trail of kisses down her neck. Jade gasped and tried to speak, but her mutterings fell on deaf ears as he removed her shirt and bra and begin licking small circles around her nipples.

Jade was startled and enjoying the moment so she decided to join in by untying the strings on Majesty's jogging pants and reaching inside of his boxers with anticipation. Majesty stopped Jade in by holding her arms with a tight embrace.

"Never do anything that you don't want to do. I don't want this situation to lead to regret!"

Jade looked up at Majesty's face and saw the sincerity in his eyes, "This is something I want. This is something I need at this moment. Let's leave all of the what ifs and questions for later."

Majesty gave Jade a slight nod and continued kissing every inch of her body. As Majesty kissed her, he moaned lightly and whispered that she tasted sweet. Jade allowed the endless tears to roll down her cheek as she allowed a complete stranger to take full control over her body. They were bittersweet tears being that Jade had never been with any other man besides King, and the fact that the same man she dedicated her life to had no more respect or love left for her.

The feel of Majesty's tongue entering her opening pulled her mind back to the right now of her life. It had been months since she felt pleasure of this kind. Majesty worked his tongue, flicking it very lightly on her spur tongue ensuring not to let his lips or tongue touch any other area. The feeling left Jade feeling defeated and she couldn't take being teased so she grabbed Majesty's head and pushed it down even further. Before he could resist, a wave of relief heartache and pain was released from Jade's body. She felt her body jerk uncontrollably and her legs instantly cross as she lay there in place, not able to move a muscle.

Majesty watched Jade lay there as a sneaky grin flashed across his face. He turned from her and removed a Magnum condom from his wallet, placing it over his erection. Jade opened her legs up for Majesty to enter as she stared into his eyes. She felt an instant connection and immediately closed her eyes to come out of the trance he had her in. Majesty made slow sweet love to her as he kissed her neck, mouth, and ears while whispering, "This shit feels so good; so right, baby."

All Jade could do at this moment was enjoy it. She had spent so much time being down and depressed over the last few years this was a release for her.

Just what the doctor ordered, she thought to herself as she heard Majesty's voice breaking her from her trance.

"I'm about to nut Jade! Oooo shit Jade!"

Majesty sped up his pace not realizing that the condom had broken from the timely session they had encountered.

"Meee too Majjj…"

Jade couldn't finish her sentence. Her body wouldn't allow her mouth to utter one sound as she went places that she had never been sexually. They both laid there out of breath and in complete awe of each other. Jade was the first to make a move, and her eyes landed right on Majesty's dick halfway covered with the condom.

"Omg, what have we just done?" Jade panicked, startling Majesty from his trance. Majesty sat up and noticed the same thing Jade had noticed seconds earlier.

"Calm down. Maybe it broke after we finished. Don't panic, baby. Everything is straight, ok?" Majesty stated trying to convince himself of this more so than her.

Jade nodded her head motioning that she would listen to him and laid in his arms as he fed her the fresh fruit that he ordered earlier.

Majesty and Jade chilled in the room for a couple more hours and talked endlessly. She felt so complete with him, although one part of her felt stupid because she had only known him for one day.

Majesty explained to Jade that he would be at the hotel for a few more weeks until the work was complete on his new home. Majesty gave Jade with all his cell numbers and his room number for her to reach him. She also gave him with her contact information and let him know of her future plans, which did not involve going back home to King right at that moment. Jade decided to give it a few hours, but she was determined to leave King ASAP.

They both left the room and went their separate ways before stealing kisses from each other while waiting for valet to retrieve their cars. Majesty car was brought out first and it made Jade do a double take. Not trying to be noticeable, she pulled her cell phone out to pretend she wasn't watching him and shot a quick text to her girls, Essence and Patience, while ignoring her many missed calls and text messages from King.

Jade: Ladies, there is something I need your opinions on. Let's meet at Essence house in 20.

Patience: In route

Essence: Ughhh. Come on; please don't let this be about King's trifling ass.

Jade: Please no judging Es, just have some drinks ready for us. O yea a pair of sweats and a tee for me as well. I had a long night.

Patience: lol y'all two are funny, stop texting and let's get there.

Essence: Whatever!

As soon as jade lifted her head from the phone, Majesty was directly in front of her.

"Everything's cool witcha?"

"Oh yes, excuse my rudeness, please," Jade chuckled and winked her eye at Majesty, as she held her arms out signaling for a hug.

Majesty obliged and held her in his arms before whispering in her ear.

"You explained your situation to me, and I'm not rushing you at all but I want you to do what's right and gone and leave what's wrong. You deserve better, Jade, so just hit my line when your problem is depleted. I will be waiting."

Jade looked up into his eyes and assured him that she was sticking to her plans; she was never going back to King again. This was the last and final straw; she finally gained the courage to leave.

They kissed each other for what felt like an eternity before valet arrived with Jade's car. Majesty ensured that Jade was in her ride safely and then he hopped into his red and black Bugatti Veyron and sped off with the latest Future hit blaring through his speakers.

Jade watched him leave; not wanting the day to end, not wanting to wake up from her fairytale. The

chirping tone of her text messages woke her up
before she could fully interpret everything that had
happened.

King: Bitch I'm going to kill you.

Jade became very nervous, frantically checking
her surroundings to ensure she saw no familiar
faces. Jade powered her phone off and smashed on
the gas; getting the hell out of dodge. She drove
straight to Essence's house for her session with the
girls.

CHAPTER 4

God wants you to become holy. -1
Thessalonians 4:3

ESSENCE

"Baby, please don't stop. I'm begging you, please don't stop," Essence panted as she sat on her kitchen countertop with one leg lifted in the air receiving some of the best head ever from her man, Real.

"Two more minutes and I'm up, so you better cum now or later," Real laughed as he stuck his fingers inside of Essence's hot spot simultaneously letting his tongue take the place of his fingers while sticking it in and out of her slowly.

"I promise I have something for you daddy if you continue longer," Essence tried to bargain with

Real's selfish ass while trying to keep her concentration on the feeling at hand. Real's licks became even fainter indicating that he was going to stop so Essence decided to take drastic measures.

She couldn't imagine him stopping, not at this moment, in fact not ever. The feeling was overwhelming so she pulled at Real's arms and told him to climb aboard.

As Real climbed on top of the marbled counter top with Essence, she slowly unhooked his belt and let his pants slide down to the floor. She positioned herself on top of him and placed all nine inches into her mouth. She still didn't feel Real budge, Real still was not going to finish what he had started with her, and that made Essence work even harder.

She slowly slid her tongue down his shaft while allowing his head to feel the back of her throat. Real panted loudly and grabbed Essence's waist; forcing her down on his face.

She decided it was her turn to tease him so she lifted up as he attempted to pull her down. She wanted him to beg to taste her juices and she knew if she continued her script, he'd be doing just that very soon.

Essence continued to allow Real's head to touch the back of her throat, each time she let it go further and further until she felt herself about to gag. Real locked his arms around her waist, this time much more tightly and cried, "Es, baby let me eat my dinner. I wanna taste that sweet shit all in my mouth."

That thug shit turned Essence on, but she still held her weight above Real's face pretending not to hear his request. When she heard Real scream that he was about to nut she let her weight fall and positioned herself directly above Real's face and allowed him to lick her like he would never be down there again. Real sucked and kissed all over Essence's spot; leaving not one drip as they both reached their peaks together.

Real turned Essence over on the counter top and made a trail of kisses run down her back. Essence screamed out in sweet agony forgetting all about the twins who were up stairs asleep.

Essence and Real loved all types of freaky shit, and they both could engage in foreplay for days. They never allowed the fact that they had kids running around the house stop them from doing them.

"Es, chill. You gon' make the boys come down."

"I can't take it baby, I can't takkkee itt…" Essence screamed as she felt the warm liquid fall freely and flow down her legs.

Real followed right behind her breathless cursing with his face all scrunched up.

"Es, round motherfucking three. Get up the stairs right now."

Essence playfully punched him as they both rested on the counter completely naked holding each other.

"Seriously though, Es, head on up stairs. I got a surprise for you."

Essence looked at Real with seriousness in her eyes. "Baby, you can't be serious. I'm too worn out. We just finished making love two times in a row.

My body is exhausted. What are you tryna do to me? Kill me?"

"Never that. Just do as I say and not as you feel so I can show you it's Real," Real rhymed to her, showing Essence one of the many different sides he possessed.

Essence jumped down from the counter and covered herself as best as she could just in case the twins came out of the entertainment room. She followed her man orders and went up the stair. She wanted to see what was so important for her to see right after having some of the most rejuvenating sex ever.

When Essence reached her room, she almost passed out from the site in front of her. She noticed a ring box on the bed along with ten tickets thrown around the box. Essence couldn't believe her eyes; she pinched herself to make sure that she wasn't dreaming.

Essence slowly approached the bed. She was weak at the knees, and didn't know if it was from the off the chain sex or the blood boiling from the view in front of her.

She went directly for the box first. The tears started that very moment as her screams became louder and muffled by her sniffling and light laughs. She slowly opened the box and the sight of the ring made her drop to her knees.

Essence fell to her bottom as she held her knees to her chest with one arm, and wiping away her tears with the other trying to get a good look at the ring.

Essence knew that Real was sitting on millions. She knew that he was that nigga when it came to being young and getting it. But she never knew he was ready to share all of that with her and her only. Essence took one more look at the 15-carat diamond and gold Lorraine Schwartz ring and smiled, thinking to herself that the ring had to be every bit of a million dollars.

After accepting the fact that all of this was real, she reached on the bed and opened one of the ten envelopes. Her mouth dropped and her hand instantly covered it but this time her scream was echoed. The invitations were absolutely beautiful.

We've decided to make it official,
We're going to tell the world that we love,
honor, and cherish each other.
Please gather with us
Essence Dupree
&
Kareem Legend
As we share our matrimonial moment on
YOU PICK THE DATE
Location: Eiffel Tower Paris, France
5 Avenue Anatole France *75007*

The twins ran into Essence's bedroom and jumped on her custom-made California Style double king sized bed while looking at her as if she were crazy.

"Mama, what's up with all the noise?" Kareem asked while looking at his mom with a smirk reminding her so much of his father.

"Yea ma, did you hit the lottery or something?" Karee questioned with anticipation in his gray eyes, which he inherited from Essence whose eyes could turn from green, gray, or blue in any moment depending on her mood.

"No boys, Mommy did not hit the lotto, and Kareem watch your mouth. Never ask me what's up with me. Mommy is just excited right now, that's all."

Real appeared in the doorway and stood back unnoticed watching his beautiful family. Real had so much to be thankful for, yet he took the credit for it all. Real reverenced himself as God because he had everything any man could want.

Real is one of the biggest suppliers down south with pills and lean being his specialty. Real valued nothing but the dollar bill. He would do anything to get it. Many questioned his greed and wondered how much was enough. They looked on with inquiring eyes thinking how a man with everything could want much more.

Real worked off pride and greed, and felt that he was untouchable. Real trusted very few in the game and ran with his cousin, Kamil, who had a face known around the different states in the US.

Real and Mil ran a lucrative business of wholesaling pills and lean to the middlemen who sold it to the street hustlers. He also flipped numbers, and had checks rolling in year round with this latest hustle in Atlanta known as free bands.

Real used to be heavy in the streets, but after years of hard work it all paid off and left him set for life. If he left the game now, he and his family could live off of their savings forever. Real was known as one of the made men in Atlanta. He was the go-to man for the hustlers that held a certain name and respect and only for those kind. He rarely dealt with small change. If he wasn't making $80,000 or better, he wasn't touching it.

Real had plans of leaving the streets after marrying Essence and sticking strictly to the numbers. He even planned on opening up a few businesses of his own which would keep the money flowing.

Real purchased three sets of condominiums for Essence, which keep her busy and entertained, gave her something to do outside of the twins and him. Essence always wanted to own a set of condos and Real always made sure that he fulfilled all of his woman's needs and made her dreams come true; no questions asked.

Essence was the landlord, and ensured that all payments were received on time monthly. She also had a team of maintenance men who ensured that all of the condos were keep up to date and good as new. The condos were located in Atlantic Station, a new area in Atlanta that smelled like nothing but green. To stay in that area stated for itself that you had some type of bread coming in, so they felt that the area was perfect for their pockets.

Kareem and Karee broke Real's train of thought as they laughed and pointed at him. Real ran over to the bed and tackled the boys.

"I told y'all li'l niggas bout that silly shit. Cut it out, boys."

The twins laughed even harder and he hugged them both while pulling Essence down on the bed with them.

Real wiped Essence tears away and looked into her eyes.

"Baby, stop all the mushy stuff. You know it's anything for you lady. I love y'all. You're all I got."

He got off the bed and slowly bent unto one knee holding the ring he purchased for her about six months ago.

Real had other situations going on in his life, but he knew where his heart was. He lived, breathed, and shit for Essence and his boys. He couldn't imagine life without the three of them. The other situations in his life didn't prevent him from making his choice because he was ready to make Essence his wife.

On his knees with glossy eyes staring at Essence in a way she had never seen, he popped the big question.

"Baby, you're my heart, my soul…everything to me," he paused a minute and gently removed a wild strand of blonde hair from her face, placing it behind her ear.

"We been down through the good, the bad, and the ugly, but now I think it's time for us to do this forever. What you say, Es? You ready to be a Legend?" Essence grabbed his hands and she slightly giggled, amused at his way of asking her to marry him. Real just couldn't conceal his hood attitude even in the comforts of their home. She often wondered if there was another side to him. She knew there was, but he did a great job at never showing it.

"Yes, I am ready to be your wife. Yes, I'm ready to add Legend to my Dupree. Mrs. Essence Dupree-Legend is a great look for me, baby."

Essence jumped on top of Real, not giving him a chance to get up from the floor. She wrapped her arms around him and locked her lips against his. Essence heard the twins laughing at them, amused by the scene that played out in front of them, but she did not break their kiss.

When Essence decided to break their kiss, she looked at her man with nothing but admiration in her eyes. She took in his smooth dark chocolate skin, his broad thick shoulders, his shoulder length dreads and become moist all of a sudden. Essence had to remind herself that the twins were there, and her soreness reminded her of the two previous sessions they just completed minutes before.

"Baby, we love you more. I'm just so excited. These tears are tears of joy." Essence rubbed her hands over his body and stared lovingly in his eyes as she explained to the boys about daddy's big surprise for them all, like they hadn't just witnessed the entire show minutes before.

The boys jumped up and down and played pillow fight as they yelled and told their parents congratulations. Real and Essence continued discussing wedding plans and called up family and friends to tell them the good news.

Real and the boys prepared for their monthly road trip by running around the house packing up clothes as if they were staying away for weeks. They used this time to build their bond. Essence admired the relationship that Real had with his boys; it made her love him even more.

"I'm going to miss my big men."

Essence was standing at the driver's side window of Real's 2013 silver BMW X1 luxury truck with chrome rims that spiced up the ride.

"No mushy stuff lady. Your men are one call away and will be safely returned Sunday by noon. Have our dinner ready and my dessert clean and ready to eat."

Essence covered her mouth and playfully punched Real in his arm.

"Really? We talk like this now in front of the boys? That's why they say whatever comes to mind, all because of their pops."

Real pulled Essence's upper body through the window and sloppily kissed her all over her face.

"So what? My boys are growing little men. They'll be straight as long as I'm around, so kill the noise.

"If you say so, Mr. Arrogant," Essence playfully joked, calling Real by the name that her brother, Reggie, gave him.

"Yea… You got it; I wouldn't want it to be any other way. Go on in the house and get ready for your li'l gossip session. Yea, I seen the messages; had to see what had you so occupied while we were celebrating. I'll call you as soon as we touch down in Florida."

Essence frowned; she hated when Real snooped in her phone. She never touched his phone because she had a strong trust for their relationship. She walked from his window and opened the back door to begin her normal kiss and hug session she gave the twins before every trip. They protested by screaming "No mom!" but their cries went unheard as she continued showering them with her love.

Essence slowly backed up from the truck and waved goodbye to her family. She felt a certain type of way about Real snooping through her phone but she wouldn't dare speak on it. He had already closed the discussion before she could even say anything about it.

What does Real have going on? The only time a nigga becomes suspicious of their woman out of the blue simply means that they have something going on; something that they're not supposed to have going on.

Essence let these thoughts digest in her mind before continuing in the house. Essence prepared herself mentally to lay the great news on her girls tonight, but she also wouldn't forget to mention Real's crazy actions.

CHAPTER 5

On a day when I am afraid, I will trust
you Lord. -Psalms 56:3

PATIENCE

Patience laid in her king sized bed debating if
she should sleep in a little longer or get up and start
her very long day. Her body felt as if it was glued to
the mattress. She rolled over onto her back and
stared blankly at the ceiling trying to prepare herself
for the long day ahead of her.

Patience was scheduled to leave Saturday
morning to attend a conference in New York,
something she wasn't too enthused about doing. Not
to mention she had to pack her clothes for the trip,
maybe even go to the mall to buy some appropriate
clothes since she didn't own anything like that.

She was drained and all she wanted to do was lay in the bed all day, but business always came first.

Patience jumped from the bed and stretched her body while yawning loudly and laughing at her own dramatic tactics. She headed for bathroom and ran hot water into her Jacuzzi style bathtub. She poured a cap full of bubble bath into the water to soothe the soreness from her body as she waited for the tub to fill.

After brushing her teeth and tying her curly hair into a ponytail, she sank into the hot water. She turned on the steam jets, which always relaxed her completely, and laid her head back on the tub headrest dozing off into another world.

****

"No...No," Patience screamed as she held her nightie down with both of her very small hands.

"Shush. I promise I won't hurt you," Mister whispered as he continued grabbing her hands and pushing them away so that he could gain access to her body.*

Patience's big bright eyes watered as she looked around the dark living room in search for someone to stop what she knew was destined to happen again.

She had allowed Mister to touch her body many times before. She knew that it wasn't right, but she never protested or told her mom because he had threatened to kill her if she ever did. Patience was familiar with this sick routine, which happened every Monday, Wednesday, and Friday for almost a year of her life.

When the abuse first started, she was shocked because Mister was around her every day. He lived with her and Hope. She later became confused; she had plenty of friends at school who she seen interact with their fathers. She saw fathers bring their daughters to school all the time and kiss them on their cheeks or forehead, but never had she seen the fathers kiss their daughters the way that Mister kissed her. After realizing that Mister was kissing her how husbands kiss their wives on TV, she became ashamed.

Patience dealt with these different emotions and the abuse until one cold night in December. This night changed her life forever; this was a night that she would never forget. Remembering that particular night gave her the courage to scream until help arrived. All she could think about was the pain, hurt, and agony she felt. She never wanted to feel that hurt again.

"Someone please help me." Patience cried out in a loud scared voice.

Mister angrily snatched her towards him covering her mouth and groping her undeveloped body parts.

"I told you that I won't hurt you again. All I want to do is touch you, so shut the fuck up!"

Patience became even more terrified at this point, and still no one appeared. She decided to take one more try. She was hoping that someone in one of the rooms would hear her and rescue her from Mister. Her screams worked this time, and she felt relieved when she saw her mother's head

appear from one of the rooms in the very large
apartment.

Her mother covered her naked body with a
stained sheet and ran over to Patience to see what
the commotion was about. Before her mother could
reach her, Mister grabbed Hope by the both of her
arms and whispered something into her ear.
Patience watched as her mother backed away from
them with tears forming in her eyes and her hand
covering her mouth.

Patience didn't know what to think or feel at
this point, so she screamed again.

"Where are you going mommy? Come back!
He's going to hurt me again."

After Hope heard her baby girl's tortured plea,
she stopped in her tracks trying her very best to
avoid any eye contact with Mister. She heard his
threat. She knew what Mister was capable of. After
all, he was the guy who stole her heart and gave her
three beautiful children. Then crushed her heart by
forcing her to give up her two sons to his older

brother Royal. Now he was trying to rape his very own daughter!

Hope just couldn't fathom the thought of taking her precious baby girl through what she knew was bound to happen. She would never be able to live with herself if she allowed Mister to take it this far.

She knew that bringing a five year old along to work with her was dangerous, but she always provided Patience with plenty of snacks, and games to keep her occupied until her night was over which was usually around three in the morning. She never imagined anyone ever trying to hurt her so she found it was convenient instead of leaving her home alone.

Hope built up enough courage to approach Mister, praying that he wouldn't kill her. The risk was worth taking to save her daughter from any harm.

"This is our child. Please don't do anything to hurt her. I'm going back into that room, and I'm going to trust that you are not that immoral. I'm going to pray that whatever piece of heart that you *have left inside of you will make you reconsider this."*

Mister smiled at Hope for a quick moment, giving her a small relief on the situation at hand. Before she could utter another word, he drew back his fist and landed it directly into Hope's jaw causing blood to splatter everywhere. Patience screamed even louder and ran to her mother's side, wiping away at her bloody face.

Mister grabbed Patience and slung her small body to the other end of the room. With tears in her eyes, Patience tried her best to get up as she watched him approach her with glossy eyes and a smirk sketched across his face.

"Help me! Help!" Patience cried out as she heard the far away sounds of sirens from outside.

****

Patience was awakened by the buzz from her iPhone. Sweat poured from her pores and she shook uncontrollably scanning the room frantically with her hands covering her body.

It took Patience a minute or two to become familiar with her surroundings again. She observed her dark shower walls and her dark shower curtains that seemed even darker at that moment. She also noticed for the first time how the curtains hung down past her dark tub, almost touching her dark tiled floor. That's when everything came back to her and she concluded that she was having another one of her horrible flashbacks. She hated reliving her past. She fought so hard to forget it, but lately she'd been having the flashbacks more frequently.

Patience thought about seeking professional help, maybe even going to church; anything to alleviate the memories from her past. At this moment, she did only what came natural. She slowly lifted her body from the tub and threw on her robe, and then she got on both knees and prayed.

Patience prayed for hours. She cried and let it all out, which actually made her feel better. This was her first time crying in years. She really couldn't remember the last time she cried. Patience didn't have any image to uphold, but she was taught to be tough and strong at a young age with no choice of her own.

Patience oiled her body down with coconut oil as she stood in front of the mirror analyzing her body. She held both breasts in her hand and slightly tilted her head to one side. She took her other hand and ran it down her neckline pretending that the hand didn't belong to her, but to her loving husband. She craved for that hand to belong to her protector; the man that would love her and accept her for her inside beauty and flaws.

Deep down, Patience longed for someone to love; for someone to love her. She wanted the fairytale relationship, which would later turn into marriage and children. The problem was, she never trusted any man enough to let him get close to her in that way. She dated from time to time, but never any men from the club. Her rule was if she didn't feel any connection on the first date then it was deuces. This left her feeling quite lonely and vulnerable because she had yet to meet a man who could keep her on her toes. No one ever held her interest, or they had absolutely nothing in common.

Patience took it as if maybe she was destined to face this cold world alone. She was only twenty-five years old, and most people her age looked at it as if they had all of the time in the world for love. Being that she never had love, not even from her own parents, foster parents, nor foster siblings, she figured she would never get it.

Time was flying and Patience knew she needed to move quickly to get everything done. She decided to dress in a very comfortable royal blue dress with knee high black riding boots. Patience removed the rubber band from her hair and let her curly hair fall loosely over her shoulders. She threw on her gray wool trench coat and proceeded to pack her bags for tonight at the club and for her trip to New York.

Patience searched her over sized closet to find her duffel bag. After searching through hundreds of bags, Patience made a mental note to clean out her closet as soon as she returned from the conference.

She walked into her all black living room, which was very small but she loved it that way. She chose all black furniture and paintings because that's basically how she felt on the inside; cold, dark, and alone. She would never let that fact be none to anyone.

Patience struggled to move the large 56" flat screen from the rack so that she could reach her hidden safe. It took her maybe thirty minutes to do so but she had no second thought about it. She removed the stacks of money from the safe and counted everything up which totaled to $30,000. That was great for one month's work at the club and she was gassed up with an instant rush for the day, knowing she was independently doing it all on her own.

Other than her monthly removals, the only time she would empty the safe was when she left her house for more than one day. She always secured her money in her savings account at Chase Bank. Patience trusted very few people. She considered her girls family so they were the only ones who knew about her stash spot.

Patience turned off all of her lights, locked everything up, and headed out of the door with her Gucci suitcase, duffel bag, and her same old pink junk bag, which held her necessities for the club. Before She before throwing her things into the trunk, she realized that her car was in need of a deep cleaning. She jumped in and headed to Fairburn Road to take her money to the bank and to let her boys clean her car at Real Deal Car Wash.

While she waited and kicked it with familiar faces, she remembered to check the email, which revived her from her nightmare earlier. The email contained all of the information for the conference in New York.

Patience Smith,

The Conference will be held at the Plaza Hotel Monday December 3, 2012. Ms.Strangler stated that she provided you with the plane ticket and information for your room. Once you arrive to the hotel, you should report to Mr. Reggie Dupree, the owner of Dupree Youth Behavioral Clinics. I would like for you to familiarize yourself with his company and their mission. You will be working along with DYBC for the remainder of your program here at Georgia State. This will give you the experience and exposure you need to successfully complete your degree.

Contact Information:
Name: Reggie Dupree
Room #: 1011
Phone: (cell) 770-897-7763
Office: (404) 619-0000

Thanks,
Scholarship Team

Patience rolled her eyes and sighed deeply, annoyed with the email she just read. She couldn't even enjoy her day because she would have to do research on the bullshit conference she didn't want to attend anyway.

College was becoming too much for her, the club was becoming something she wanted to rid herself of, and life was just a revolving cycle altogether. No excitement at all. At this point, she concluded that she wasn't living, she only existed.

Patience decided to complete her research while she waited for them to finish up with her car. Her research consisted of her running a quick Google check on Mr. Reggie Dupree. She found herself somewhat interested in his company. She loved his mission to transform the lives of youth and the goals and future plans he had for his company. Her degree was actually the same as his and his company was somewhere she could see herself working.

Maybe this idea wasn't bad after all. Maybe this was a dream come true. I wonder how this Mr. Reggie looks. He's probably some stuck up old black dude with a stick up his ass. Patience laughed at herself as she came up with crazy thought after crazy thought about her new volunteer venture.

Patience pulled up to Essence's house in the Cascades and saw Jade getting out of her brand spanking new Lexus G50. Jade had a weary look plastered on her face. Patience prayed that everything was okay with her girl. Patience continued to the trunk for her workbag because she planned to get dressed at Essence's spot to avoid the locker room and King for her performance tonight.

"Look at you black beauty! These hoes don't stand a chance with you. When did King buy this for you and where is the Magnum?"

Jade cringed at the mention of King's name. She wanted to tell the story one time and one time only so she told Patience to hold her horses so that she could relive the past all in one breath.

The ladies both walked to Essence's door. She was there to greet them before they had the chance to let themselves in. Essences threw an invitation in their hands and begin giving them the rundown of everything. The ladies were all so energized at this point. Jade and Patience sipped on their wine and Essence smoked tree after tree while the extra large theater sized TV watched them talk, laugh and make lists of plans for the wedding.

This was their usual spot when it came down to getting all of the weekly drama off their chests. The theater in Essence and Real's multimillion dollar home held all of their secrets, successes, dreams, and nightmares.

Jade used this time to forget all of her problems and drown herself in the joys of her best friend's great news. She was so happy for Essence. She felt that it was about time Real tied the knot with her girl.

King had once told Jade some very disturbing news, but she didn't believe him. Jade would always brag about Essence and Real's relationship to King, which would make King very angry. King downplayed her girl and Real one particular night, but Jade just couldn't believe him. King and Jade didn't have a very trusting relationship at all; it was more like they were in a competition rather than a relationship, so she always brushed his negative comments off as a way not to change for them to become better.

"So what is the emergency?" Patience eagerly asked, while applying her lip-gloss to every inch of her juicy plump lips.

"Y'all know I have to be at the hellhole in two hours. Plus, I have some news to catch you ladies up on as well, so run your mouth black beauty."

Jade looked at both of her friends with her innocent eyes and dropped her head into her lap. Patience, being the more affectionate one when it came to her girls, ran over and patted Jade on her back motivating her to go ahead with her story.

Jade explained everything; starting with the purchase of her new Lexus, her seeing King have sex with one of the strippers, her heading to a hotel to stay for the night, to her meeting and sexing a complete stranger. Jade explained to the girls about how he made her feel, which was a feeling completely new to her. She told them every single detail, leaving nothing to the imagination about her night with Majesty.

Everyone sat there dazed for a moment with blank expressions on their faces. Essence pulled her blunt for a bit too long, and the girls laughed as she coughed uncontrollably before trying to speak on the drama that was just presented.

"So bitch, you mean to tell me you sucking and fucking on the first night? King always cheats; that ain't nothing. Don't let me find out Ms. Innocent over there is a closet freak."

Jade looked at Essence out of the corner of her eyes and retorted, "I had to ask myself that too, because this was a side of me that I didn't know exist. Don't judge me y'all, but I think I love it."

Patience spit her wine out in a state of pure disbelief, walked up to Jade, and pretended to check her temperature.

"Is this Jade? Jade Jones? The reserved, *I will never cheat on my man*, Jade?"

The ladies burst out into laughter again, not believing that Jade had finally come out of her tightly shut box.

"So what's next?" Patience continued. "You going back to King again after this? Everything was placed right in front of you this time, no hearsay at all."

Jade parted her lips to speak but before she could form her words, Essence interrupted her.

"Fuck yea; this bitch is going back to his ass. It took her long enough to get the balls to cheat and repay his sorry ass, but you better believe it's gone take ten more years for her to finally leave."

Jade smiled slightly, simply ignoring Essence bluntness as thoughts of Majesty flooded her brain. She could still smell his cologne lingering through the air, and she could still envision his lips attached to her body.

The laughter of the girls snapped her back into her reality.

"No, not this time ladies," Jade replied. "I think it's time for me to live a little. It's time for me to do what I have to do for me. I know it's gonna be hard since King is my source of income, but I do know that it's not impossible."

Patience placed her arms around Jade's shoulder. "Beauty, you know we have your back. Money should never be a reason to stay in an uncompromising situation. Essence is rich, and I'm living so you know what's ours is ultimately yours."

Essence didn't feel the need to play the supportive friend role. "So you mean to tell me that just because Superman whispered all of these sweet nothings in your ear, ate your little goodies, and helped you get over the fact that you saw your man fucking another woman, you finally leaving now?"

Essence attitude was just her way of caring. It was the only way she knew to express herself. She not only thought, but often times quoted how she was God's gift to the world. Essence was drowned in money, living the good life, honoring money, cars, and anything luxurious. She had it all and thought that she would never lose it. She loved to throw that fact in everyone's faces.

Jade rose from her spot in the theater to pour another shot of wine, she needed some time to ponder on Essence's question. "To answer your question, Essence, I'm doing this for me. Not everyone is as strong as you are. Yes, it took me a while to wake up, but I never thought you would throw it up in my face."

Essence began to speak, but Jade stood stopped her. , "Let me finish, please. You always have the limelight and the time to speak. Now it's my time. I have been through hell and back with King, but it's my story not something that should be thrown around as a big joke to you. Not everyone was blessed with a great man like yours, but count your blessings not my problems because all things have a way of changing."

Jade grabbed her purse and keys. "I'll hit y'all later. I'm out."

Patience and Essence sat there with their mouths almost touching the floor. They couldn't believe the new person Jade had turned into overnight. This new person was amazing to Patience, but Essence wasn't too keen of the new Jade at all.

"Whatever, I just tell it like I see it and nothing will be changing between Real and I anytime soon."

Essence contemplated her last statement before the words even fell from her lips. It totally slipped her mind to tell her girls about his suspicious behavior.

Patience begged Jade to wait a minute while she quickly put them up to speed about her trip to NYC for the weekend. The girls being in their own feelings at the moment let Patience words go in one ear and out the other. Essence was so caught up in a childish staring match with Jade that she didn't even hear Patience mention that she would be working with Reggie Dupree at Dupree Youth Behavioral Clinics.

Patience tried to lighten up the atmosphere with her strong positive spirit, but it didn't work so she decided to get dressed and leave after Jade for her last night of work for the week.

Patience pulled up to Magic around midnight, late as usual, but she didn't care. She locked her things in her trunk and headed to the club's entrance dressed in her attire for the night with an ankle length tie around mink covering her body.

When she entered the club, the loud music and the stench from the mixtures of smoke entered her nostrils causing her to frown a bit. She made her way back into the locker room and placed her mink in her closet.

King wasn't good for much, but he did keep his workers happy due to the upscale nature of his clubs. Most strip joints had locker rooms that were as filthy as an alley in the hood. Not King spots; all five of his clubs were laid completely out, spacious and immaculate which drew attention from ballers all around the country.

Just as Patience was leaving, she overheard Diamond and Red discussing the events of yesterday so she walked over to them to get the scoop. Her sudden presence shocked both of the girls because they knew Patience didn't fuck around in the club. She was in and out, no questions asked, nor conversations started.

"Yes, she stormed out of here like a mad woman. It was fucked up to say the least, but King's ass is off the chain. She's too pretty to put up with his shit," Diamond spoke while eyeing Patience sideways trying to figure out why she was interested in their conversation.

Patience broke the silence. "So who was it?"

Red looked at Diamond as if she needed permission to speak and Patience shook her head in utter disgust at the grown women in front of her and repeated herself.

"Who was it?"

Diamond smiled and gave Red a nod signaling for her to go ahead with the drama. Red looked around the locker room and whispered, "It was Tri, they say she and King been kicking it since she started a couple months ago."

Patience slightly nodded her head and walked off from Diamond and Red. She received the information she needed, and her job with the dummies, as she called them, was done. She heard Diamond utter something slick, but she paid her no mind as she proceeded to the stage for her usual performance.

Every Friday night she would grace the stage with her and make a quick ten bands. She normally performed the same show, and showed a tad bit of skin to the hungry regulars to keep them enticed. Patience was good at what she did; sporting some of the sexiest lingerie and the most expensive heels just added to her already natural touch. She was unique, there were no other dancers like her, and that's what drew in the fans and the continuous dollars.

Patience drowned downed three shots of Patron that one of the trusted bartenders brought her as she swayed her body to the beat of the music behind the curtains.

The wine from earlier and the Patron shots relaxed her completely and she felt at ease. Patience tied her hair into a very high ponytail letting the long strands of her curly hair hang down to the middle of her neck touching the tattoo of her Chinese peace symbol.

Patience turned her body positioning it in front of the mirrors, which were wall to wall in Club Magic. She smiled in admiration for the first time in a long time, maybe it was the alcohol talking to her, or maybe she was just stunned at her own striking beauty.

As the curtains rolled down, Patience stood face to face with the patrons, bartenders, servers, and the bouncers. She completely blocked them all out, pretending to be the only one present in the room.

The patrons were in total awe of Patience; many new clients would come out just to see her perform on Friday nights. This night the club was packed to capacity; holding almost four hundred people in the building. Patience knew exactly what that meant and that exited her even more.

Patience walked out slowly and seductively in her gold spiked seven inch Christian Louboutins, which gave her short figure a very sexy appeal. The gold garter complimented her caramel toned legs as it set right above the scripture tattoo on her thigh. Her red romper accentuated her caramel skin causing her to have a distinct glow about herself. The romper showed off her midsection from between her chest down to her panty line leaving the onlookers yelling and throwing cash her way just from their pure excitement.

Patience took in the words from "Never Seen", a hit by a new up and coming artist in Atlanta named Shaka. The music was exclusive, made especially for the strip joints, which was the type of music she preferred while on stage.

The lyrics and the alcohol allowed her body to bounce to the beat as she climbed the pole and slid down back first into a split landing in front of twenties, fifties, and hundreds. Money was flooding the stage even flying down from the balcony VIP section of the club. The loud music continued to flood the speakers as Patience continued her performance.

After Patience's performance, she headed to the locker room to count her cash and grab her belongings. As soon as she entered, she heard Tri's loud voice slick chumping on the encounter she had with King.

"Yea I continued fucking him right in front of that slob ass bitch of his. So what? Ain't nobody checking me, so all of this talk can really be ceased. It's such a waste of breath to discuss what's already understood. Y'all bitches are really messy. new subject please."

Patience approached Tri like a bat out of hell when she heard the disrespect drip from her mouth about Jade. Patience grabbed Tri from behind and slammed her head into the mirror in front of her station. Tri fell to the floor and she looked around drowsily trying to figure out what in the hell had just happened. Patience stomped her one time in the stomach.

"You're right; talking is reckless, especially when it comes to my family. I have no problem with what you choose to do with him, but bitch you will respect my family by all means."

Tri grabbed the stool in front of her station to assist her with standing while all of the other dancers in the room looked on shocked as hell. They had never seen Patience step outside of her box of being the classy one. The girls whispered and laughed at Tri while one of them ran to notify Trick of what just went down. He came running to the locker room to stop the commotion before things got out of hand.

Tri stood and looked at her bloody reflection in the cracked mirror. She wiped the blood away from her lips and turned around.

"P, you really just snuck me like that? You of all people?"

Patience snarled her lips causing her dimple to form a slight smirk in her cheeks.

"No words remember? Next time, watch your mouth."

Patience rolled her eyes and walked off headed for the closet to get her mink and car keys. She was heated and ready to get the hell out of the club so she could prepare herself for her trip. When she turned, Tri was standing directly in her face and Trick was entering through the doors.

"Watch your back!" Tri threatened as she pointed her bloody finger in Patience face.

Patience looked at Tri and laughed, "Looks like you need to do a better job at watching yours, freaky!"

The ladies in the locker room broke out into roars of loud laughter, creating an even bigger scene. The little scene was soon cut short as the crowds begin to disperse due to Trick's loud demands.

"Clear this damn room now, y'all better get y'all shit together before you get sent home."

Patience looked back at Trick and shot him a mean bird as she continued to King's office only to see that he was gone for the night.

I guess he's going to see why Jade's ass hasn't been home, Patience thought to herself as a slight smile appeared on her face being so proud of her girl for finally deciding to leave King's dog ass alone.

Patience fought her way through the crowded club as she ignored the stares and weak game of the thirsty niggas there. Patience exhaled once she made it outside. The cold air brushed against her body as she tried to cover up with the coat she failed to put on before leaving out.

In route to her car, she noticed a black on black BMW truck parking next to her car. She rushed to get inside before the occupant of the vehicle could see her, she didn't want any run-ins with anybody, not tonight anyway. Once she made it inside of the car she pulled out her cell to dial her girl up to tell her the drama that had just unfolded, but didn't get an answer. She figured that Jade was still angry from the argument with Essence earlier. Patience was so eager to get the drama off her chest so she decided to call Essence.

Essence answered on the first ring, but before Patience could speak, she was startled by a slight knock at her window.

"Hello, hello…" Essence screamed through the phone. "I know your ass not drunk playing and shit on my line, Patience?"

Patience laughed at her silly friend and told her to hold on a second. She rolled down her window slowly creating a small crack to rely her message to the guy who knocked. Before he could even speak, before he could even get a good glimpse at her Patience interrupted him, "Have a great night sir. Whatever it is, I'm not interested at all!"

She sped off leaving him standing there without a second thought about it. She retrieved her phone from the passenger's seat.

"You better still be on this line, Es!"

"I'm here bitch, what's up?" Essence replied, slightly annoyed at her crazy ass friend.

She never understood why Patience didn't give guys a chance. Sometimes she thought that Patience was going to be single and lonely forever due to her past.

Patience explained everything to Essence about her night, even about her driving off on the guy in the black truck. Essence couldn't believe Patience was out there fighting, especially without her being present. Patience continued talking to Essence as she drove like a bat out of hell to the airport trying her best to make her flight. Essence stressed the issue that Patience needed to start dating and stop pushing people away from her. Patience didn't want to hear that nonsense so she ended the call and turned her music up as loud as it could go; blasting Keyshia Cole's new album.

CHAPTER 6

Great men are not always wise. -Job
32:9

REGGIE

Reggie landed at John F. Kennedy airport in
NYC bright and early Saturday morning. He headed
to Enterprise Rent-A-Car to pick up his rental, then
straight to the Plaza Hotel to unpack and get
prepared for his meeting with the Georgia State
intern.

Reggie took in the breathtaking view in front of
him realizing how content he was to be away from
the "A" for a while. White snow covered the
ground, and the birds flew high in the sky as the
traffic flow and busy people continued on their
daily journeys. The man made pond across the
street was frozen solid and the surrounding
buildings were dripped with snow, which made him

envision the movie Home Alone and other movies filmed where he stood.

The freezing cold wind deterred his desires to sightsee and the heavy luggage didn't make things any better so he headed to his room to take a short nap. Reggie rested for a few good minutes before his ringing room phone awakened him.

Who in the hell could have my room number and why so early? Reggie thought to himself as he lazily reached for the phone.

"Reggie," he answered in a raspy voice.

"Um, yes this is Patience...Patience Smith, the intern student from Georgia State. I did not receive a time or a location for the meeting you wanted to have with me today."

Reggie lifted his tired body up from the comfortable king sized bed and became fully awoke at the beautiful sound of her voice.

Wow, if she looks anything like she sounds then we're going to have a serious problem.

"Look, I'm sorry about that. I had my assistant draft an email with details, but I'm guessing she never got around to sending it. You're at the Plaza Hotel too, right?"

"Yes, I'm in room 2107,"Patience responded becoming eager to see the face behind the sexy voice.

"Cool. Meet me in the lobby at ten sharp and we will go from there. Dress warm because this isn't the "A." It's freezing out here," Reggie joked causing them both to chuckle lightly before ending the call.

Reggie decided to arrive in the lobby a little before ten. He didn't want to be late, and he was definitely curious about this woman for some reason. Reggie looked at his reflection in the glass and gave himself a grin, pleased at what he saw staring back at him.

Reggie's 6'2 muscular athletic build stood out from anyone else in the crowd that morning. His khaki colored Michael Kors suit matched perfectly with his mocha colored skin. He wore his dreads braided into a ponytail, which gave him a rugged-business appeal.

He stood at the end of the front desk nervously biting his bottom lip, a habit he had for years. He looked at his Breitling to check the time. It was ten on the dot, which caused an unfamiliar nervousness to overcome him. Before he had a chance to look up and prepare himself, Patience appeared before his eyes.

"Hello, I'm Patience Smith." Patience extended her hand to introduce herself. "I'm guessing that you are the infamous Reggie Dupree?"

Reggie eyes could have popped from the sockets as he was stunned by the beauty in front of him. He smiled while taking Patience's hand and blessing it with a kiss. The soft unexpected kiss caused Patience to blush slightly, something that she rarely did. Reggie caught the blush, but before he could really cherish the moment, Patience quickly straightened her face and displayed a very serious look.

"Yes, that would be me, Ms. Smith. You look absolutely…I mean, you look very nice. May I lead the way? We're going to continue this at the coffee shop down the street from here, if that's okay with you."

Patience held Reggie's strong gaze and nodded her head yes. "That would be great, but only under one condition."

Reggie continued to stare at Patience, almost burning a hole into her light brown eyes. His eyes then lowered to her juicy plump lips that held a beautiful beauty mark right above. He was simply stunned. Minutes passed before he actually spoke.

"Anything, just say the word."

Patience eyes landed on her hand; the hand that Reggie still held in his, "If I can have my hand back!"

Reggie apologized as he held the door open for Patience, signaling for her to head in the direction of their meeting. Reggie was all into his thoughts on their way to Zena's Coffee shop, which caused the walk to be rather short and detached; not that he was expecting an attachment anyhow. It was as if they both were in thinking mode, not even realizing the other's presence.

Reggie slowed his pace so that he could take a little more of Patience in without her noticing. He was in complete awe at the lady who stood only inches from him; this was something surprising and completely new to him being that he normally didn't feel connections with women often. He came across beautiful women daily, but none of them had him startled to the point of nervousness. Reggie, being a newly renewed businessman, endured his rough street days and nervousness wasn't becoming of him. There was something he couldn't quite put his finger on about her, but he definitely knew he was interested.

Once they arrived at the coffee shop, they both reached for the door handle at the same time. Patience, not wanting to be the one to back down, pulled at the door but was unable to open it all the way. Reggie overpowered her causing her to be taken back because she was accustomed to all of the power.

"I got it, Ms. Independent. When you're with me, I'll be the one to open doors, pull out chairs, and make sure you're comfortable."

Patience smiled a very uncomfortable smile feeling defeated yet again as she allowed Reggie to open the door for her, and pull out her chair once seated at a table inside. They both ordered and silence stole the floor as they waited for the server to return with their orders.

"So tell me about yourself. This doesn't seem like the line of work that you'd be interested in, better yet owning?" Patience asked as she subconsciously judged the businessman/thug in front of her.

Reggie tilted his head to the side and squinted his face up a little, astonished by her question. A lady had never insulted him in such a blunt manner as Patience had. In fact, all of the women loved him and would flock to him like birds to a piece of bread.

This woman intrigued him. She was sure of herself, and her qualities were being revealed all at once during their first encounter. She was a challenge. He liked her so he decided to put Patience up to speed on his life story. He had no idea why, but he wanted her to become familiar with the real Reggie, not just the businessman.

Reggie straightened his face and began to nod his head back and forth before speaking.

"I'mma let you in on the inside scoop about me. I never want you to misinterpret me based on my looks so are you ready, Ms. Smith?"

Patience held up her wrist showing off her rose gold JBW watch.

"We have nothing but time on our hands. The conference isn't until Monday, right? So, it's just me and you."

Reggie liked the sound of what Patience hinted on. He liked the way she carried herself, and he loved that he didn't intimidate her. He even felt like a different man just from being in her presence. It made him uncomfortable but he would stay uncomfortable to experience more of her.

Reggie gave Patience the run down on his life. He told Patience about his childhood and how he watched his parents struggle; working job to job just to keep food on the table for him and his sister. He explained how his childhood caused him to jump head first into the streets. The money he made in the streets was enough for him to retire. He didn't believe in greed, and he didn't believe in free so he invested his money in his first three chains of behavioral health clinics for the youth.

He explained to her how those eight clinics made him millions and also gave back to the community so he decided to expand purchasing twelve more clinics in other states. He went over goals for all of the clinics and he also explained to Patience about the different programs Dupree Youth Behavioral Clinics offered.

He provided Patience with a copy of all of the paperwork that her college had her previously fill out to ensure she was approved to intern for his company by the state. He presented her with her temporary nametag and gave her paperwork for her state issued ID that he would order as soon as they got back to the city. Reggie enlightened Patience on what most of the conferences were like, and he provided her with case files on audited clients that she would have to familiarize herself with.

After spending over an hour introducing parts of his life and business to Patience, he felt as if he were in a counseling session. Reggie normally left training to his staff so that left him no room to really just personally know his employees and vice versa. He always kept business and work separate, but something was drawing him to Patience, something that allowed him to convince her that he was worth the intern.

Patience adjusted herself in her seat and cleared her throat after being somewhat amazed at Reggie's story.

"Wow. I apologize for my judgmental remarks earlier. You can never judge a book by its cover, huh? I reference that saying to my life a lot so it's necessary I allow others that same respect.

"No need for apologies; I totally understand. Being in this line of work, I have learned to judge from a point of discernment. We never know what a person has been through. We never know what causes a person's future actions."

Patience replied with a simple, "true" and finished her cappuccino, which had been refilled for the third time. Patience was really enjoying Reggie's company; it scared her because she had never truly enjoyed the company from the opposite sex before. Patience would blame it on her past or just blame it on her not being interested. She always tested the waters and tried to build relations with men, but it just wasn't there.

She stared at him as she continued listening to his positive intellect. She found him to be sexy and very intelligent. She noticed his thick lips; lips of a GOD with tattoos covering what looks to be his entire body causing him to look like a piece of art. She took in his dreads, his broad shoulders, and his beautiful face. She had never seen a man with such a beautiful face, a face that spoke measures.

His Tom Ford Italian Cypress cologne was etched in her nostrils causing her to smell only him, not even her strong cappuccino in front of her. Patience jumped up, being shaken from her daze when he grabbed her hand.

"Huh…what happened?"

Reggie smirked, realizing that she was just as lost in her thoughts as he was.

"Nothing happened. The waiter is here. Would you like to order anything else before we leave?"

Patience slowly removed her hand from his embrace for the second time and grabbed for her wallet while stuttering.

"No…um, no I'm just fine. How much did everything come to?"

"Twenty dollars," the waiter replied.

Reggie frowned and looked at Patience sideways.

"What's up? What I tell you earlier?"

He turned his attention to the waiter handing her his black card and applying her tip to the receipt.

"What was that about? I'm capable of paying for my own and possibly yours too!" Patience snapped at Reggie, hating the feeling of being overpowered by a man, as she stood implying that she was ready to leave.

Reggie ignored her attitude and simply stated. "I already told you how it works when you're with me. No ifs about that, so just get used to it. You will be around, right?"

Patience ignored his question and placed her hands on her hips causing Reggie to laugh at her animated behavior. Reggie retrieved his card back from the waiter and decided that it was time for them to head in separate directions. They exited the coffee shop just as they entered with Reggie walking a bit slower taking pleasure in the moment at hand without Patience knowing.

Nighttime rolled around quickly or either the business meeting lasted longer than Reggie expected; whatever it was, he just couldn't shake the feeling Patience gave him. It had been eight hours since he last seen her, eight hours since the first time he laid eyes on her and he really felt a certain kind of way.

His hardcore demeanor felt a bit softer when around her. He felt as if he could open up to her. He knew that she would soon be receiving her Masters in Counseling; he held that same degree. He personally knew doctors who worked in the field of Counseling and not once did he feel the urge to express himself. She made him think about things that he knew should never cross his mind due to the fact that their relationship was about business and business only. Reggie was an ex street guy that knew the downfalls of mixing business with pleasure and he didn't want to experience that now or ever, but somehow he knew it was coming near.

Reggie showered and dressed in a red YSL shirt along with a pair of YSL dark denims. He decided on his wheat Timberland boots and his YSL hoodie to keep him warm in the freezing weather. He looked in the mirror and wondered if Patience found him attractive. He was headed out for drinks to help the night pass by and ole girl was still on his mind. He grinned cockily and said to himself, *Hell yea, she know I'm that nigga. It's gone take a while to break her though. She's headstrong as hell, but I'll be patient for Ms. Patience.*

The sound of his annoying iPhone ring tone interrupted his pep talk. He was a bit disappointed until he saw Essence's name and the twins' picture flash across the screen.

"What's up, sis? Where the boys at?"

"Dang, I can't get no love? I'm the one who called you, not the boys. At least see how I'm doing first," Essence whined like the spoiled brat that she always was.

Reggie laughed at his baby sister. "Shut up and man up. I don't wanna hear that baby shit. It's not all about you."

Essence smacked her teeth and replied, "Well I'm hanging up then. Bye."

Reggie knew that Essence was dead serious about hanging up on him, so he gave in to her spoiled ways. He told her to hold on while he locked up the room. He put Essence up to speed on his trip to New York, and she beamed with delight as she told him how proud she was to have a big brother like him.

Essence told him about the wedding and how Real surprised her with everything. She already knew Real ran it by her brother because they were very close; had been since Reggie's street days.

"So why didn't you tell me? I know Real already told you about the wedding?" Essence picked at her brother.

"Es I could never ruin that mans secret. I'm no rat so you gotta go search for cheese elsewhere. Besides, you too fucking spoiled. I gotta take my hand out the cookie jar with your ass. From now on, I'm only riding hard for the Kareem Junior and Karee. You really getting out of hand, especially if you think I'm putting you up on game 'bout what my partner discusses with me."

Essence continued to gripe; this time being more playful. "So that's how you doing it with your only sister? I don't believe you, so it's all irrelevant."

Reggie burst out into laughter. "You see what I'm saying? I'mma show yo ass. Get off my line. I'll holla at you when I'm back in the city."

Essence couldn't compose herself any longer as she also burst out into laughter, loving the way they both knew what to expect from the other. He begged her not to hang up earlier, and now the tables had turned and she was begging him not hang up.

"My friend, P, went down to New York this weekend too; something about volunteering or some shit. Hopefully y'all meet up down there. I swear, y'all two would be great for one another. Omg, y'all definitely would be! I'm introducing you to her at my surprise party that Real is throwing for me next Saturday. You thought I didn't know, huh? Yea, I figured that out all by myself."

Reggie listened to his sister chat as he walked inside of the Oak Bar inside of the Plaza to relax and rewind a little.

"Kudos. I'm glad you did your dirty work on your own this time. What else did you find out? Did you find out about the new Bugatti he bought you?"

Reggie laughed hysterically because his sister didn't respond to his joke.

"For the record, I'm good sis. No need to play the dating game with big bro. I'm managing just fine."

Essence broke her toughness and laughed too.

"Convince me, because I can't hear you. You will definitely meet P at my party, baby boy, so come ready.

They stayed on the line a bit longer catching up on the twins and discussing their plans with their parents. Reggie was now downing his second drink enjoying the conversation until he noticed that distinct laugh, a laugh that was so unfamiliar yet so transparent to him. He followed the sound and his eyes led him to a bar stool in the far left corner of the bar.

He could have sworn his eyes were playing tricks on him. Patience was chopping it up with a nigga that he knew from back in the A. All types of thoughts flooded his mind as he stared blankly with no expression.

Is this who she traveled to New York with? Is this her man? How does she know him?

Essence's whiny voice interrupted Reggie's thoughts.

"Why are you ignoring me? I know you didn't hang up in my face?"

Reggie stood up, grabbed his drink, and told Essence to hit him later. She refused, so he politely hung up in her face. He knew that she would blow up his phone until he answered again, but Essence was the last thing on his mind.

Reggie discreetly moved to the side of the bar where Patience sat, sitting close enough to hear her and dude's conversation. He didn't know what prompted his bizarre behavior; he didn't even know why he cared.

Once he was close enough, he took in her view from the backside. Patience was dressed in a black and white polka dot dress that was fitted to her upper body and flared out at the waist giving her the appearance of a doll. She wore her hair in a curly bun with the natural brown strands seeping from the back. Her caramel tanned legs were thickly proportioned and very toned as if she played sports for a living. The six-inch black diamond studded Maddens she wore made her appear taller than he remembered. She was stunning, she was beautiful, and right then and there Reggie knew that she was the missing ingredient in his life.

Reggie realized that he needed a woman in his life, but not just any woman. He needed a woman who could hold him down and bring out a side of him that he never knew existed. He never considered this until he meet Patience. Seeing her sitting at the bar with a man and not knowing their status made all type of feelings emerge from him.

Reggie took in her view and drowned in the sweet smell of her perfume as he listened in on the two.

"So, is the answer yes?" the dude asked Patience. "I don't take rejection lightly."

Patience sighed. "I'm not into dating right now. I told you this back home. I don't like repeating myself."

"Damn, Patience," he replied. "You always shooting niggas down. You must like women."

Reggie shifted in his seat, eager to hear Patience's answer. Was that the reason she acted so funny in the coffee shop?

Patience rolled her eyes at her suitor. "That is precisely why I can't deal. All of you guys are the same. Just because a woman doesn't want you, doesn't mean she's gay. If it makes your ego feel better, then yes, I'm gay. You can go now," she casually dismissed the dude. "I was enjoying my alone time before you arrived."

Although he admired her spunk, Reggie had to laugh at his old partner. Dude was still trying even though Patience was done with the entire conversation.

"Look," she hissed. "I don't need anything from you or anyone else. Since you can't seem to take a hint, I'll just excuse myself. Goddamn," she uttered.

One part of Reggie was elated that Patience wasn't in New York with buddy; another part of him was raging because buddy was still grilling her and she had already told him what was up. Reggie replayed what the guy said over and over in his mind.

"Look at this. All of this can be yours if you just say the word. Look at what you doing back home. It can be a guaranteed check if you just fuck with me."

What the fuck did he mean by that? What exactly was Patience doing back home besides college? All type of questions flooded his mind. He wanted to know more about her, but because the interest he had in her was personal he would have to do his own personal research.

The sound of Patience yell broke his thoughts.

"Never, and I mean never touch me like that again!" Patience stood up from the bar stool with her finger pointed against the guy's forehead.

Before the guy could react and remove her finger, Reggie appeared right next to Patience's side. Reggie didn't have to say a word; his presence spoke measures. Dude was stunned as if he had just seen a ghost.

"Regg, what's up? What the hell you doing all the way up here?" Dude nervously spoke as he retrieved his coat from the stool, scoping out his surroundings for an escape route.

Reggie's jaw muscles flexed as he pushed Patience behind him, forcing her to remove her finger from dude's head.

"My whereabouts don't concern you. Matter of fact, we not discussing me at this moment; we're discussing you. I think it'll be best if you just leave. The lady said she didn't want to be bothered."

"Oh yea…yea… I was just leaving. Wasn't I, Patience?" Dude nervously asked, hoping that she would back him up.

He knew the code of the streets. He knew that Reggie was a deadly man, and he did not want to cross those lines.

"Correct. We were both just leaving," Patience harshly spoke as she pushed Reggie's arm aside and regained her spot back directly in front of dude.

Dude was literally shitting bricks. He didn't know what kind of game Patience was playing, but he didn't want any parts of it. Sweat poured from his pores. He wiped them away as he tried his best to watch Reggie's next move.

Patience grabbed Dude's arm and intertwined it with hers as she lead their way out of the bar leaving Reggie stunned at her actions. Reggie drew his arms up in surrender as he noticed Dude's constant frightened stares shooting back at him as they walked out.

Embarrassment wasn't a term that Reggie was familiar with so this feeling was something new. It angered him, but he was a very composed man so no one even noticed. The bar patrons looked his way, confused at the scene that they had witnessed, but he completely blocked them all out. He downed shot after shot with nothing but thoughts of Patience on his mind.

CHAPTER 7

Like a dog that returns to its vomit, is
a fool who repeats his foolish actions.

-Proverbs 26:11

JADE

Jade couldn't believe the nerve of Essence. She
often questioned their friendship due to her
insensitive behavior. Essence's beauty and her
materialistic nature went far beyond her head. She
felt that everyone was beneath her. Jade was tired of
being on the defense with this so-called friendship
they had. Jade drifted back to a time when their
relationship was beneficial to her. She wanted to
remember the times when there were no millions,
no Real, no twins, and no egotistical Essence.

****

Before Jade moved to Philly, she and Essence were inseparable. They were both on the same cheerleading squad from kids at Adamsville Recreation all the way to preteens at Jean Childs Young Middle School. They would attend school dressed alike, and practically did everything together from double birthday parties to double dating.

Even when Jade was forced to move away due to her mother insecurities about her father, she would still come back to Atlanta to visit Essence and her other family members over the summer and on some holidays. They would hang out until the wee hours of the night partying at the Pool Palace, which at the time was a local club in Atlanta where everybody who was anybody attended. The girls made it their business to hit up Cascade Skating Rink; they were even featured in the movie the rapper T.I shot there called "ATL."

Jade and Essence were more like sisters than friends, and Reggie took Jade right under his wing, making sure she were always straight. Jade's life wasn't perfect, but it definitely wasn't horrible...not until she met King. She remembered meeting him like it yesterday; those memories along with the ones of her parents were stuck with her forever.

After Jade witnessed the brutal murder-suicide of her mother and father, she was sent back to Atlanta to live with her mother's sister, Aunt Bell. Jade was stuck receiving counseling four days out of the week which cut her chances of doing what she loved, and that was cheering. This resulted in Jade spending her days cooped in the house eating everything in sight or hanging out with Essence at whatever party or event that was hot at the moment. Essence was something like a release for Jade. Essence allowed her to be herself and they built a bond stronger than before during that time.

The girls had one more week left in school; one more week before officially being high school graduates and they didn't know what to do. Essence was the popular one due to her looks and the luxurious clothing her brother, Reggie, provided her with so the girls took this to their advantage, and decided to throw a party. They figured what better way to be remembered, and it also allowed them to make a few extra bucks by charging a door fee.

They passed out invitations to all of the seniors and a few popular under classmen during that week. The rest of the week, they worked on decorations, and getting a DJ to host their party. Reggie helped the girls out by renting an old club building on Bankhead and providing the party with loads of alcohol and weed.

The night of the party had arrived and to say that the girls were happy would be an understatement. The party was packed with hundreds of people, including some of Reggie's homeboys. There was so much food; from hot wings, nachos, and any other party food that you could name! Everyone seemed to be enjoying themselves.

Since Jade didn't drink or smoke, she sat off in the corner eating a plate of hot wings and nachos. She sat in the same spot all night, bobbing her head to the music, in her own little world until a very handsome guy interrupted her.

"What's up? Why you ducked off in the cut like this?"

Jade nervously wiped her mouth with a napkin and stumbled over her words.

"I'm just…I'm just having a little fun to myself, I guess."

King laughed; he was feeling the black beauty that sat before him.

"I'm King. And you are?"

Jade looked around, almost in a panic, and prayed that Essence or anybody would interrupt their conversation. King felt a rush from her shyness. He knew that he had to have her; something about her innocence turned him on. He wanted to get to know her, but to do so, he had to make her feel more comfortable. He sat down across from her.

"There's no need to be scared. I promise I won't bite you."

Jade was still very much nervous and she was definitely unsure of what he wanted with her. She brushed her long bone straight black hair back with her hands and built up enough courage to speak. "Hi… My name is Jade Jones. I'm 17 years old and a senior at Benjamin E. Mays High School. I just moved back to Atlanta a few years ago and I basically stay to myself unless I'm with my best friend, Essence."

"Ok, li'l mama. I'm one of Reggie's homeboys. Didn't you say his sister was your best friend?"

Jade slowly shook her head up and down, "Yes, she's my best friend, and Reggie is like a brother to me. How come I never seen you around?"

King pulled on his blunt and coughed lightly before answering.

"I'm a very busy man, so consider yourself lucky, baby girl, because I'm making time for you."

Jade blushed, enjoying his company and not to mention his looks. King stood 6'4 with a tall and slender frame. He wore his hair in a low cut curly fade, which complimented his deep dimples in both cheeks. Handsome would be an understatement. Jade totally forgot that she was throwing the party because hours slipped by as she talked to King all night long.

That day and every day afterwards, they became glued to the hip. King meet Jade's aunt, and although she didn't approve of his age nor his belligerent behavior, she decided to let Jade date him. Aunt Bell knew that King was a man with plenty of money. She figured anything was better than her spending her hard-earned money on counseling sessions for Jade.

Aunt Bell was absolutely correct about her assumptions and later happy for her decision to let Jade date him due to King paying the rent and other utilities for them. Whatever Aunt Bell needed, King provided it, trying his best to keep her happy for the sake of keeping Jade around.

For Jade's graduation present, King surprised her with a 2006 Dodge Magnum on twenty-four inch rims. King showered her with gifts, took her on trips all around the world, and made her forget her issues for the moment. Jade believed that King was a blessing from above and she submitted to him in so many ways than one. They eventually moved in together sharing their first few years of bliss with each other.

****

After leaving Essence's house Friday night Jade wanted to be anywhere besides home. She contemplated on getting a room; she really could've used some personal time to reflect on the last couple of days. Jade decided to do just that so she headed back to the W hotel. To her surprise, Majesty had already notified the front desk to direct her to his room if she came back.

Jade was drained and ready to lie down so she swiftly stuck the card key into the door but it wouldn't budge. She tried this process three more times before deciding to take the long trip back to the front desk to curse them out for the inconvenience.

As Jade turned around to walk towards the elevator the door swung open and someone pulled her in from behind. Jade screamed, not knowing what the hell was going on as she tried her best to claw at the person's hand.

"Shhh…beautiful it's me, calm down," Majesty whispered in Jade's ear. He then placed the tip of her ear in his mouth and playfully nibbled on it.

Moans escaped from Jade's mouth as she attempted to turn her body around to face him. When her attempt was successful the tired feeling which consumed her body before was replaced by pure lust at the sight of his chocolate chiseled chest that was cut as if he lived in the gym.

Jade played the aggressive role this time as she pulled his head down closer to her mouth and engulfed his lips into hers. They kissed at the door for what seemed like hours before Majesty lifted her in the air and swung her around. Jade automatically became self-conscious by his actions and decided to step back into her reserved box. Majesty noticed her reactions and broke the silence by complimenting her.

"You look even sexier than before, baby. I want you to stay with me."

Jade blushed as she pulled at her shirt making sure that it was down.

"Thank you. You are handsome yourself; not to mention very slick too. How in the world did I end up here again anyway?"

Majesty pleaded his case to Jade while giving her the puppy dog eyes and soft expressions. He then offered to take Jade to pick up a few things to wear since she didn't have any bags with her. They both decided to head to Wal-Mart where they purchased nightwear and snacks for the room. Majesty practically begged Jade to spend the weekend with him, which didn't require much convincing at all.

They spent day in and day out in the room enjoying each other's company. Jade was forced to turn off her cell phone due to the constant phone calls and texts she received from King. She blocked the entire world out and made this weekend all about her for a chance.

Majesty was Jade's new release. She was able to step outside of her box with him and try things she would never imagine. She was enjoying the feeling of freedom, and the respect that came with Majesty. She enjoyed his company so much that Monday rolled around and she didn't even want to leave. She knew that it was time to end this thing with King for once and for all, so she dressed before Majesty awoke and headed out.

Today was the day that she would finally end her unlovable relationship with King for good. She knew that he would want the keys back to the new Lexus he had purchased for her. She also knew that he would keep all of her possessions. He'd probably make her walk out of the house naked as the day she was born.

King was heartless like that; he was a self-centered bastard with no feelings or emotions at all. Jade vowed that whatever the outcome was, she would be proud of herself. This was something essential to her growth as a woman. She wouldn't waste another minute of her life playing the fool for King.

Jade pulled up to their condo in the Historical West End area of Atlanta. Before she prepared herself for war with King, she wanted to talk to the one person who had helped her through the last few days. Jade removed her Samsung Galaxy Tablet from the AUX cord in her car and dialed Majesty's number. The phone rang once before his powerful voice blared through the speakers.

"Why did you leave without telling me? Is everything good? Do you need me?"

Jade's smile spread across her face. She couldn't believe how attentive Majesty was to her wants and needs. Jade was so comfortable with being showered with money and possessions to make up for the time and attention King lacked, she didn't know how to genuinely accept Majesty's gestures.

"Thank you so much for the support you're giving me," Jade sobbed lightly and wiped at her tears before continuing. "This is so hard for me, but I'm doing it, baby, I'm doing it now. I have no idea what my outcome will be but none of that even matters."

"Look, I'm here for you. Day four and I'm not going anywhere. Let that nigga have all that shit. You'll get it back times ten, believe it. I'mma be on standby. I want you to call me in an hour. Shoot me another number to check up on you just in case you don't hit me."

Jade tears streamed down her face and she hesitated before calling out Patience's digits.

"This is my girl P's number. Hit her line if you need to, but I'm sure everything will be fine.

Majesty was quiet on the other end. He was trying to process everything that had happened over the last couple of days. He didn't know exactly what it was about Jade, but whatever it was gave him reason to stick around knowing her situation.

"Cool… one hour flat and I'm calling. Matter of fact, give me the address. I'm coming if I don't hear from you!" Majesty demanded, going with his natural instincts considering everything that Jade had expressed about ole boy.

Majesty wanted to know info on him, but Jade refused to get into full detail. It boggled him that he didn't know the man behind the woman he was growing on. He would never forgive himself if he allowed Jade to be harmed by him.

Jade fumbled with her bag as she hit the button on her keys to lock up her car. She stopped in her footsteps when she realized what Majesty had requested of her. She wasn't quite ready to reveal the identity of the man she constantly allowed to hurt her. She wasn't ready to be embarrassed anymore than she had already been, so she chose to keep his identity a secret to Majesty.

Majesty had this distinctiveness about himself, something she was growing to love. No way in a thousand years would she want him to know about her weakness. She wanted Majesty's behavior to continue; not change based on her past so she ended the call by promising to call him as soon as she ended things with King.

Jade entered the condo and the smell of weed smoke filled her lungs causing her to cough uncontrollably. She heard the sound of Rocko's latest hit blaring through the house as she neared the bedroom. When she entered, she was caught off guard at the sight before her. The same chick that she caught King with was on top of him, riding him backwards. Neither King nor the chick noticed Jade's presence as they panted and moaned.

Jade was past furious; she felt disrespected in a major way and the feeling was incomparable to any other that she had ever experienced. As the tears rapidly fell from her eyes, she quickly wiped them away as she silently talked to herself.

This is what I deserve? I can't believe he stooped this low and brought his bitch to our home, in our bed. If I wasn't sure about leaving him before, this is the icing on top of the icing on the cake.

Jade's eyes landed on King's gun, which was on the dresser adjacent to the bed. She didn't care if they noticed her; to be honest she didn't have a care in the world as she blankly headed towards the dresser to retrieve the gun. She fired one shot from the Glock nine, which caught their attention.

"What the fuck…!" King cursed as he consciously reached for the Desert Eagle he kept concealed on the bedside as he jumped up aiming straight for Jade's head.

Tri sat at the top of the bed, knees to her chest and tears streaming from her eyes. She was caught up in a love quarrel and she was frightened; not knowing what to do or say for the second time within a week. She knew that her involvement was wrong. She was fully aware of King and Jade's relationship. She figured if he didn't respect it, why should she? Now she was reconsidering it all as she sat there stunned, not knowing if her life would end at that moment as the warm liquids fell freely down her legs.

"Bitch, have you lost your fucking mind?" King shouted as he ran towards Jade.

He knocked the gun from her hand and grabbed her long hair.

"Look at yourself!" he yelled as he turned her to face the mirror before slamming her head into the glass; shattering the glass.

Jade didn't scream nor cry; she was numb to the pain that was being inflicted upon her. Her nonchalance pissed King off so he continued slamming her head repeatedly until the screams from Tri knocked him out of his daze.

"Please, King, just stop. You don't want to do this. It's not worth it. Let's just leave!"

Tri was standing behind King trying her best to free Jade from his deadly grip. King flinched causing Tri to fall back and hit her head against the edge of the footboard, which knocked her unconscious. Tri's attempt allowed Jade a release from King's grip. As she crawled towards the

Glock, she was blinded by the blood pouring from her head.

She didn't feel the need to scream, she didn't even feel the need to call for help. She just wanted King to suffer as she had for so many years. The vast amount of blood that she was losing caused her to become woozy. She could feel the gun in her hand, but her vision was blurry as she squeezed the trigger praying that she would hit King. Shots rang from the gun but she didn't hear any screams. She didn't hear any footsteps, nor did she feel any pain being afflicted upon her. She figured that King had fled. As she rose from the ground, she dizzily made her way into the bathroom before she felt a piercing pain shoot through her back causing her to pass out on the floor.

CHAPTER 8

We must obey God rather than men. –
Acts 5:29

ESSENCE

Essence had finally allowed her body to rest
after staying up all night reading "Thicker Than
Water 2," by her favorite author, Takerra Allen. She
spent her weekend cleaning the house and doing
major numbers on Real's credit cards due to her
boredom. Real and the boys were still out of town
and she was missing them like crazy. Not to
mention her girl, Patience, was out of town on
business and she had argued with Jade, which left
her going crazy in zombie land. Her only options
were to read and shop so she did just that all
weekend long.

Essence snuggled up with her zebra print
comforter enjoying the smell of Real's cologne,

which was etched into the material. She could've sworn that she was dreaming but the smell was becoming stronger and the bed was becoming warmer as she sleepily moved around. Essence fought with her body and her mind because she had finally drifted off into a good night's rest and she would hate to end her sleep only to find out that her man really wasn't there.

She felt soft kisses on her face, which slowly moved to her neck and then lowered to her chest, which caused her to slowly open her eyes. She smiled noticing that it wasn't a dream after all. Her man was home, and she was relieved to know that her boys were safe.

Essence often dreaded to see them leave knowing the lifestyle Real lived. She knew that Real possessed power in the streets, but she also knew that with power came pain. Essence worshiped the ground that Real walked on, reverencing him as King above all men, even God himself. She felt that with everything she and her family possessed without having a relationship with

God, what good would it do to build one with him now.

"Baby, when did you get here?" Essence whispered in a raspy sleepy tone as she wiped the sleep from her eyes.

Real continued his kisses, ignoring her questions, and causing her to moan and crawl from under the covers.

"You like that, huh? Tell daddy that it feels good!"

"It feels good, daddy. I missed you and I need you," Essence revealed as she returned kisses to Real's chocolate toned body.

She positioned herself behind Real grabbing at his broad thick shoulders, massaging them as much as she could with her soft small hands. She took turns massaging his shoulders and playing in his shoulder length dreads, which he wore in a band allowing them to hang onto the tip of his collar. Real rotated his neck allowing the pleasure to seep through his upper body as he took her feet into his hands and rubbed them lightly.

Real had been gone for two days to long and he was in need of Essence. He craved her and only her, despite his lifestyle in the streets, a lifestyle that involved money, women, and more women. Real lifted Essence from behind him and positioned her forward on his lap. He sucked and bit on her neck causing her red skin to redden even more as soft whimpers escaped from her mouth. He loved to leave love marks all over her body. It reminded him that she was all his. They continued their foreplay, simply enjoying the fact that they were back in each other's arms where they both belonged. Essence straddled Real until she couldn't take anymore, causing them both to fall asleep in the same position.

Essence awoke that next morning before the guys so she decided to treat them to a light breakfast before dropping the twins off at school. After cooking, she showered and dressed in a tan and orange off the shoulder Chanel sweater with tan leggings, wanting to be comfy for her many meetings today.

She was visiting the leasing offices of the three condominiums she owned, which she did throughout the month to ensure that everything was being managed properly. Her face was familiar to the residents and the person managing her properties; that was something she made sure she maintained.

Essence rushed into Karee's room, jumped into his bed, and showered him with kisses. His loud laughs woke up Kareem who came running into the room right behind Essence to join the fun. They continued enjoying each other's kisses before Real peeked his head into the door ruining the moment.

"Aye Es, what I tell you bout all them kisses? We got little men here, not dolls!"

Essence threw Karee's football pillow at Real, catching him off guard. "These are my babies Real…we can kiss each other all day every day and they will remain our little men! You must be jealous? Daddy wants some love too?"

"Daddy already had some love, you haven't forgotten have you?" Real joked as he walked into the room to join the fun with the trio.

After their morning episode of kisses, hugs and pillow fights, Essence instructed the twins to go into their adjacent bathrooms to shower and get dressed for school. Essence laid out their clothes for the day, which were identical just as they were, but switched up their shoe game. Essence laid out the white and red Bally's for Karee and the blue and red Bally's for Kareem, which would make their school uniforms pop.

Essence and Real decided to let the twins attend private schools for right now, providing them with something different educational wise was something they both wanted. Essence loved Real with her all, but her boys were her heart. She didn't know what she would do without them. They kept her sane and they definitely kept her going on days she wanted to give up.

Kareem and Karee were two little matching bodies with different minds and characteristics.

Karee had a lighter complexion, but not as light as Essence, and he was very composed compared to his brother. Kareem took after his father with the darker colored skin tone and the very outspoken attitude, which were two of the reasons they decided to make him a Jr. The twins loved their parents to death despite the exposure their dad introduced them to at such an early age.

As much as Real tried to convince himself that they were little men, their little hearts wouldn't allow them to grow up so fast. They could never be as mature as Real trained them to be on a daily. He realized this fact could have been beneficial to him on this particular morning.

Once everyone was dressed, they all headed in the direction of their nose and stomachs which led them directly into the kitchen. They all sat at the bar and enjoyed their breakfast of waffles, boiled eggs, and turkey sausages.

The boys engaged in light conversation about their little trip to Florida as Real rudely talked on the phone with his cousin Mil, catching up on a little business. Essence was literally in her own little world; dazed off enjoying her breakfast and the company of her family until she replayed her son words in her head over and over again.

Karee: "I can't believe you were scared, not big bad Kareem!"

Kareem: "I wasn't, it's just… I didn't want to hurt her, she is our little sister."

Karee: "Shush…are you crazy."

Kareem: "Not my sister, but you know what I meant."

Essence replayed the dialogue between her boys until every single word soaked into her memory. She looked around the table at her family. She dropped her fork, causing everyone to stop and look at her. She nervously bent down to pick up the fork and that's when she noticed the weary behavior and stares from the twins. Kareem rushed out of the kitchen and waited at the door for his mom and brother. If he had never been ready to get out of the house and head to school, he was that day.

Essence would never approach her boys about such a trivial matter, but she definitely would make a mental note to bring it to Real's attention. Essence dropped the boys off at school and did her landlord duties, visiting all three properties in Atlantic Station, which took up most of her mental space for the time. She made certain that all tickets placed by residents were completed. She completed her monthly checklist, and she signed rights over to buyers who had successfully paid off their properties.

Even though she was working, she was unfocused. She desperately needed someone to talk to. She needed her girls right now, so decided to head over to Jade's house to apologize about their disagreement from the other night.

Essence never took the time out to need or want God. She never even mentioned him even during her time of need. She had no idea that God could make everyone unavailable for you so that you could become available for him. She had no idea that God could make her world crumble right before her eyes, and none of her money would be of any assistance to her. Essence lived in a world where money, possessions, and family proved to be number one to her, and she did not intend to change that.

As Essence approached the Sky Lofts, she noticed yellow tape and police cars lined up and down the street. The entrance to the condo was blocked off so Essence parked on the side of the street and jogged all the way to Jade's door, wanting to know the juice, wanting to take her mind off her own problems.

Out of breath and feet aching from the jog, she finally reached Jade's door but was redirected by an officer.

"I'm sorry M'am, but we are securing this area for evidence purposes. Can you please leave from this floor?"

Essence became worried as she took in the officer's words

"Um… my sister lives here. Please tell me that she is fine!"

The old smug looking black officer studied Essence's body as if she were a piece of fine art work, totally ignoring her comment. This angered Essence causing her naturally green eyes to turn gray and her hands to shake uncontrollably as she ran further down the hall to the other officers.

"What in the hell happened here? Someone tell me something...anything! My sister lives here!"

A very handsome younger guy appearing to be the detective on the scene wearing slacks, suspenders and a white button up shirt that hung loosely out of his pants walked up to Essence and grabbed her shoulders attempting to calm her down.

"Hello m'am, I'm detective Estrada. I can't give you too much information, but I can say that we escorted two females to the hospital in an ambulance. Can I have your name and your relation to the homeowner?"

Essence blankly answered all of the detective's questions and took his card before running off down the hall heading to her car. Essence called Patience and told her to meet her at Grady leaving out full details, not wanting Patience to become emotional and fall into one of her infamous states of depression.

After hanging up with Patience, Essence called her parents and put them up to speed on the events of the day. Her mother offered to get the twins from school and take them to the house to pack their bags up for a few days. She knew that Essence would want to be there for Jade. Essence declined her mother's help, but Mrs. Cynthia Dupree was firm when it came to her word and she wouldn't have it any other way. Essence needed this time to be there for Jade and to confront Real without the twins being present. Therefore, she decided to let her mom have her way.

Essence arrived at the hospital in ten minutes flat; leaving her platinum Audi S8 parked directly in front of the building, ignoring the security officer threats to tow her car away. She ran to the information booth that sat directly in the middle lower level of the hospital and frantically gave them all of Jade's information.

While she waited on the worker to check the hospital's system. She searched through her messages and call log to ensure that she hadn't received any missed calls or text from Jade that morning. Seeing that she didn't, Essence repeatedly dialed Jade's cell number almost thirty times before eventually preparing herself to call Real to get King's number.

The phone rang once before Real's loud baritone voice exploded through the phone's speaker.

"Es, you do that now? Don't answer when I call you? Have you lost your fucking mind?"

Essence frowned, remembering the problem at hand, which was more important than the drama that she would speak to him about later. She had been ignoring Real's calls the entire day, not knowing what or how to replay what she had overheard to him.

"I think Jade is in the hospital. I went to her house and police were everywhere. They told me that two females were rushed to the hospital. I'm here now and I need you to get in touch with King for me. I will let you know the details when I know what's up."

Real's voice lowered after hearing the news. "What! Let me get him on the line! Make sure you hit me soon as you get word. Es, answer the damn phone when I call you too."

Essence ended the call as soon as Real was done speaking. She wasn't sure if she was going to grant his request to answer his calls anyhow. She knew that her actions were childish, but it was her way of dealing with things that she really preferred not to deal with.

Essence was becoming irritable due to the slow workers at the information desk and just as she was about to go in, the chubby bald worker interrupted her.

"M'am, it seems that we do have a Jade Jones here. She was admitted here this morning. My system is showing that she is currently in an emergency surgery."

Essence eyes watered instantly after hearing the news. So many different thoughts flooded her brain causing many questions to fly from her mouth and she wanted answers now. The worker was familiar with this irrational behavior from families, so he calmly looked at Essence through the top of his bifocals and gave her directions.

"You can head down to the first floor to the ICU unit's waiting area. I'm sure someone can help you there."

Essence ran towards the elevator in panic mode, pressing the elevator button continuously and ignoring the same security officer that had followed her into the hospital.

"M'am, I can see that you are in a hurry, but I would hate to see that nice car get towed at the expense of you not moving it to another area."

Essence mind was gone at that moment as she threw the officer the keys, demanding that he move the car for her. The officer stood there in pure shock, he had never driven an expensive car before, matter of fact he hadn't driven a car in quite a while now. The large smile on his face quickly vanished as he remembered that he was working at Grady and not Emory. They didn't allow visitors the luxury of valet parking.

"Umm… I'm so sorry, M'am. We don't offer valet parking here!"

The sound of the elevator's doors opening gave her relief as she dug in her large Michel Kors handbag in search for her wallet. She threw the officer a crisp hundred-dollar bill and winked her eye as she instructed him on where to bring her keys once he was done.

Essence arrived on the first floor and was completely pissed off again knowing that she would have to wait yet again before anyone would tell her information on Jade's condition. She offered the nurse money just as she did with the officer and just as she thought the underpaid nurse happily took the money and told her that she would have an update as soon as they did a shift change.

The security officer returned with Essence keys with a gleam in his eyes that she didn't notice before. He thanked her for the opportunity and the cash, but she was too zoned out to even reply to his sentiments. The wait alone gave her time to think of her own problems again, something she was trying so hard to place in the back of her mind. She was so caught up in her thoughts she didn't see nor hear Patience enter the waiting area.

"Es, what in the hell is going on?" Patience asked for the third time in a row as she pulled at Essence's arm to break her from her trance.

Essence wiped away at the tears that had formed and proceeded to explain everything she knew about Jade's condition so far. Before she could finish putting Patience up to speed on her days events, Real unexpectedly arrived. Essence couldn't muster up enough strength to look at Real without breaking down so she discreetly looked away. Real noticed Essence's distant glare although she thought he didn't. he knew that she was scared for Jade, but the look she gave him, and the unanswered calls let him know that it was much more going on with Essence than just that.

CHAPTER 9

Nothing completely covered will
remain covered and nothing hidden will
remain unknown. –Luke 12:2

PATIENCE

Patience fretfully sat in the waiting room of Grady's intensive care unit with so much on her mind. She had no idea who broke into her apartment. She had not one detail on what had happened to her Jade, and to top things off she was still having horrible nightmares about her past.

Patience arrived home Monday morning after her long weekend in New York to a door practically knocked off the hinges. Her living room, which was once decorated with all attractive black fixtures, was destroyed. Her sofas were cut completely up, and newly man-made holes decorated her once collaged walls. The safe had been sawed from behind her 56' flat screen and pieces of the television covered the floor.

The local pigs bombarded her with loads of questions as if she was involved in the robbery of her home, which made her blood boil even worse. Their jealous stares stood noticed as they wondered to themselves how a college student could afford all of the extravagance she possessed. They provided Patience with little to no insight on the perpetrators, and they left her in the blind on the entire process at hand as she rushed to get them out of her busted home after receiving the terrifying call from Essence.

Patience didn't stress over the loss she had just encountered because everything that those fools destroyed were replaceable. What bothered her was the fact that she couldn't put her finger on who would have the desire to break into her place. She beat herself up as she half listened to Essence talk about irrelevant topics, but to no avail. She was still left with no answers on either of the problems at hand.

"I can't believe this shit, P. you keep a thin line between business and pleasure, and hell your dull ass have no pleasure anyway, so who in the hell could have targeted you?" Essence asked as she looked at Patience, waiting for a reply.

Patience sneered her top lip causing her dimples to appear while shaking her head.

"Exactly! My business is school and Magic, and my pleasure is nonexistent so that leaves one of the two. Either someone from school or someone from the club, and I know it wasn't school."

"Well, we have our answer then…" Essence stated before stopping short in her sentence because someone distracted her.

Patience followed Essence's eyes and they landed directly on Real as he walked towards them, causing silence to spread throughout the waiting room. Real greeted them with hugs and he flooded Essence with kisses down her neckline. He showered her with compliments and got no reaction from his fiancée. Patience and Real noticed

Essence's apprehension and Real being the more blunt of the two decided to speak on it,

"What's the update on Jade, and what the fuck is wrong with you?" Real's loud voice broke the silence as he sat in the empty seat next to Essence, receiving upset stares from the other visitors.

Essence nervously looked away and looked down to speak, updating Real on what she knew so far which was nothing and avoiding his question about her behavior.

Patience noticed the tension between the two so she stepped away to make a few phone calls. Her first call was to King. She had major questions for him; mainly she wanted to know why he wasn't at the hospital while Jade was in ICU for God knows what. King's phone rung once and went straight to voicemail which shocked Patience. She left a message letting him know the deal on his girl.

Patience was starting to grow a strong hate towards King due to his disrespect at the club and the lack of respect he had for Jade. Thoughts flooded Patience's mind before her ringing phone brought her back to the present.

How could his black ass not be here? I hope he's not responsible for this shit.

Patience looked at her phone's caller ID and was hesitant to answer because the phone number was unrecognizable. She let the phone continue to ring for about three times before answering with a very dry, *"Hello."*

"Aye…Is this P? Ya girl, Jade, gave me your number earlier and instructed me to call if I couldn't get in touch with her. I'm a little worried because I been ringing her since our last call a couple hours ago and still nothing back."

Patience removed the phone from her ear and took a closer look at the phone number to see if she could identify it yet again before responding.

"Who is this?"

"I'm Majesty, one of Jade's friend's. Is she straight?"

Patience became very nervous at this point, which caused her defenses to kick in, "Why wouldn't she be straight? Did you do this to her?"

"Did I do what to her? Where in the hell is she? I need to know that everything is good with her. Can you please tell me where she is? I'll explain everything once I'm there."

Patience was reluctant, but at the same time, she knew that Jade had mentioned this new friend of hers to them. She wondered just how close these two had gotten; how much did this Majesty know about her life with King. As she paced back and forth forgetting that Majesty was still on the line, so many different scenarios replayed in her mind.

Did Jade plan on leaving King and things didn't work out as planned? Did Jade discuss her plans with Majesty? Did Majesty do this to her?

"Aye P, are you still there?" Majesty yelled causing Patience to snap out of her daze.

"Um Yea, I'm here… come to Grady Hospital ICU. We will discuss everything when you get here."

Patience hung up with Majesty and leaned over the railing that sat in the middle of each floor in the large hospital. She looked down to the bottom level and watched blankly as different people came and went to. She was in deep thought, and seeping into depression at that very moment as her thoughts took her back to when she first meet her best friends after graduating high school back in 2006.

Just like clockwork, Patience's phone vibrated in her hand, breaking her trance and almost causing her to drop it down below where she once stared. After regaining the balance in her hands she realized that a message had came through from an unfamiliar number. Once she read the text, her thoughts took her back a few nights before. They instantly took her back to New York.

404-202-3434: What up P? Been thinking bout ya since NY. Can we get up later? My flight lands at 8.

Patience stared absurdly at the text message; she couldn't believe that Dude really used her number. It was all just a game to her and she definitely didn't want him to think otherwise. The night when Reggie approached them in the hotel and tried to control her situation, she became angry. She didn't know what it was about Reggie, but she definitely knew that she didn't need anyone controlling things in her life except for her.

Being around him made her feel weak. He intimidated Patience, but she would never admit to it. His masculine demeanor and his dominance spoke measures. That was something so new for Patience; something that she had never experienced from a man before.

She was determined to put her powers into use that night at the bar. She wanted Reggie to know that she was a big girl and could take care of herself just fine. When Reggie approached her and Dude, trying to assist her with getting Dude out of her face, she switched sides on him quickly.

She told Reggie that she and Dude were just leaving and she sexily marched right out of the bar arm in arm with Dude who was in total shock. She noticed the nervous look plastered on Dudes face, and she could tell that Dude was relieved at her boldness, which led her to believe that Reggie held some sort of rank in the city.

She didn't know of Reggie's reputation, in fact she had never seen him back home in Atlanta. If it wasn't for the internship her college appointed for her, she would have never known he existed. She knew that overruling him would prove to be too much for his ego, but she did so with much pride indeed.

Unbeknownst to her, he had something in store for her as well, that's why she was back home so early with no insight on her intern duties at all. She couldn't believe her eyes when she awoke this morning; a simple message was placed on the door along with new flight information for her.

Meeting is canceled and your start date at the office is:

Wednesday, December 5, 2012 @8 sharp.

Reggie

Patience looked back at the text message from Dude again and laughed to herself while thinking,

After a day like this, I could use some pampering from a little nobody. Besides, it's been forever since I've been out, so let's see how this plays out."

Patience replied to his message, taking control as usual, letting him know when and where they would meet. After her simple reply, she looked over at Essence and Real to see if things had calmed down between the two before heading back over to tell them about the phone call she had just received.

In the middle of her explaining what transpired over the phone with Majesty, the nurse appeared with a very disturbed look on her face. All of the guests in the waiting area puckered up from their weary positions not knowing who she was coming out to speak to.

A sense of relief washed over their faces when they noticed that she was headed in another's family direction. As soon as Patience continued to speak, the nurse that Essence bargained with was approaching them with a doctor by her side along with a very handsome new face added to the group.

"Hello, my name is Dr. Todd, are you the family of Ms. Jade Jones?" the bulky young doctor asked, as he nervously peered at the petrified faces in front of him.

"Yes…" they all spoke in unison, everybody except for Essence, and the handsome guy that appeared with the doctor.

Essence and Mr. handsome just stared at one another for what seemed like minutes as they all looked on in anticipation. Real was becoming heated at the pure disrespect right before his eyes, but he decided to save the drama for later and stay on the matter at hand; Jade's condition.

"Ok great," the doctor interrupted the awkward silence between the group and continued. "Let me start off by saying that Jade is a very strong young lady; she and the baby are true fighters. She was beaten very badly and shot in her lower back with the bullet not entering. The bullet pierced her back, causing third degree burns and fragmentation to the skin surrounding the wound. She lost a lot of blood mainly due to the severity of the beating, but we stopped the bleeding and ensured that it wasn't internal. Her condition is stable but we aren't allowing anyone to go back until further notice. We're keeping her under very close watch to ensure that she doesn't drift into a coma. She's been going in and out of consciousness since her arrival, so we have a sit in nurse monitoring her at all times.

Everyone stood there completely astonished from the news they had received. They couldn't believe that she had been beaten, shot, and left for dead, nor could they believe she was pregnant. After hearing the news, Patience had a suspect in mind, and she couldn't wait to see him.

They continued their discussion with the doctor, loading him with question after question feeding their curiosity. He answered all of what he could and informed them that a detective would be in to speak with them shortly.

When the nurse and doctor walked off, Mr. Handsome nervously introduced himself to the crowd, "I'm Majesty, Jade's friend. I got here as fast as I could especially after calling her phone repeatedly with no answer." Majesty went on to explain how he and Jade meet and how she gave him the inside scoop on her relationship, promising to break things off with the guy.

They all listened intently before Patience loaded him with many questions, feeling some sort of relief with every answer that he gave. Majesty respectfully answered everything, understanding her concern about her friend's relationship with him; he wanted to be as informative as he could.

Essence didn't say a word, she just watched him with a look of disbelief on her face. Her own problems with Real were obsolete at this point and all she could do was stare Majesty down. Real sat back with the look of death on his face watching Essence watch another nigga. He had never seen that look on Essence face before and it caused him to be on edge. He tried to maintain his self-control, but it was all going out of the window as he grabbed Essence by her arm and pulled her towards the elevator.

"You on some real disrespectful shit, so I'mma step before I do something I just may regret."

Hearing Real's voice brought her back to her right now. She had totally blacked out after seeing Majesty. It had been exactly five years since the last time she seen him, and what was mind-boggling to her was that their last run-in was in the exact same place they stood now, *Grady Hospital*. Essence knew that her reaction to seeing him didn't look too good, especially if Real felt the need to approach her about it when that was so out of character for him.

Essence turned her body around to face Real, which caused him to loosen up his grip on her arm.

She hugged him and freely ran her fingers through his dreads causing his defenses to drop just a little. She looked into his eyes; seconds away from revealing secrets from her past, until she remembered her promising future with him and her boys which caused the words from her heart to disappear and the words from her mind to flow freely.

"No disrespect at all, Real!" her shaky voice sniveled. "We don't do the disrespect thing so you know it had to be something deeper behind the stare," she continued.

Real looked into her eyes noticing the slight change of color, he knew that she was in her feelings because her eyes changed colors in the midst of pressure. He knew his woman like a book, just as she figured she knew him in return. What they didn't know was that even after spending years together and developing a family, they both held their own little hidden betrayals.

Real broke the embrace and moved back slowly from her, pressing the down button on the elevator, "I'm out…you can finish up your little stare down. We'll finish this up at the house."

Essence didn't protest at all. In fact, she was happy to see him leave because she was seconds away from tears. She couldn't believe her fate, especially during a time like this. She was in disbelief about so much that she finally allowed the tears to fall freely from her face. Patience approached her friend with open arms and an open heart without inquiring about her problems at all; and that's exactly what Essence needed.

Patience, Essence, and Majesty sat in complete silence as they waited for the detectives to arrive. Patience noticed the tension in the room and was just about to speak when they noticed three detectives enter.

"I'm detective Estrada. I see we meet again," the detective said while approaching Essence to shake her hand.

Essence politely shook his hand, ignoring his previous comment; she was ready to find King's ass and have him killed at this point.

The other two detectives noticed the anxiety in the room and the larger of the two spoke up.

"Um, we would like to individually interview the three of you about Jade Jones."

They all obliged and went their separate ways with each of the detectives; ready to hear all of the details involving Jade's incident. After spending over an hour interviewing, they reunited to continue the interview as one large group.

Patience couldn't believe that there was someone else involved who was also hospitalized. When detectives stated the female's name, she automatically knew that King was behind this entire ordeal.

Patience was furious as she shook uncontrollably while trying her best to explain everything to the detectives about King's possible whereabouts. She gave them the name of all five of his clubs and anything else she could think of. To her surprise, the detectives had already had everything on him including leads to his whereabouts.

Majesty was present in the flesh but his mind was all over the place. He couldn't believe his eyes or ears. First, he sees Essence after almost five years, and then he finds out that King was the guy that Jade failed to reveal to him.

Did she already know about our connection? Is that why she refused to reveal his name to me? Did he really do this foul shit to her? Is Essence really a big part of Jade's life?

So many thoughts ran through his mind, but none outweighed the fact that he had developed feelings for Jade. He was so in over his head at this point that stepping away from her was not an option. He thought of how different things would be if everything came out about his past, and then he quickly dismissed those thoughts from his mind as he made a promise to never let any of it be known to her.

Patience life was so out of order during the last past days which caused the week to fly by as fast as ever. Wednesday had crept up on her so fast, and she was the least bit prepared for her first day of internship. She groggily lifted her drained body from the bed and pulled her cell phone from the charger, sending Dude a quick text message. He replied back within seconds, not even allowing her to check her missed calls or other text messages. She had no energy to be angered by his behavior, in fact she found him amusing and quite thirsty. Their dinner date and light shopping from the other day was exactly what she expected from him. He was boring and not challenging at all, as he bragged and constantly flashed his money around. Dude was a complete turnoff, but she chose to let him stick around for the convenience.

Patience: Come and scoop me in 1hr.you're my chauffer for the day!
Dude: No Problemo!

She was in no mood to drive today, so she figured he was just the person to have around. After nipping that in the bud with Dude, she called the hospital to check in on Jade's condition, which turned out to be a waste of time. The nurses weren't allowed to give her any information over the phone.

Patience couldn't grasp the scenario in her head of how Jade was laid up in the hospital, and not to mention the unknown pregnancy that the doctor informed them of. She wanted so badly at that moment to be with her girl; to retaliate against King and anybody else involved in the drama. She couldn't though; it was all out of her control so she dropped to her knees and prayed a prayer of healing and restoration for her friend.

After showering and dressing comfortably in her black and red Armani plaid sweater dress she searched through her shambled shoe wear for a comfortable shoe that would accentuate her outfit. After looking for twenty minutes too long, she settled for a pair of black Armani low cut heels. She didn't want to overdue herself so she went very light on the jewelry and accessories wearing her hair wild and curly all over. After applying her normal line of Mac to her lips, she sprayed a light coat of *Daisy* by Marc Jacobs on and admired herself in the mirror.

She took a quick look around at her new spacious condo and smiled to herself. Essence had really looked out for her with this one; another reason why she loved her girls so much. Patience became comfortable in her new spot in no time, but she would be fooling herself if she denied missing her old spot a little. She couldn't risk spending another night in her apartment, especially with the police closing the case claiming not to have any evidence. So once she got word she simply contacted her insurance company with the info on her damaged and stolen belongings, then she contacted DFACS to notify them of the incident. It took them no time to approve her new location, which was a condo in one of the buildings Essence owned, and her $30,000 check would be rolling in by the end of week to compensate her for the damages.

Patience was grateful to say the least because things could have definitely been worse for her. Patience locked up her new condo and headed to the front to meet Dude, while thinking of her misfortune and her blessing in disguise. *"Everything that seems bad isn't always bad."*

CHAPTER 10

But if we hope for what we do not yet have, we wait for it patiently. – Romans 8:25

REGGIE

Reggie sat back in is Ezno leather recliner with both feet propped on the ottoman in deep thought. The ottoman set in the middle of his living room, offsetting the other pieces of furniture that decorated his simple home. Reggie's home was very masculine and basic; he preferred it that way since he was the only occupant and the only guest besides close family.

His bachelor pad base colors were royal blue with a soft hint of red, which were two of his favorite colors that he wore quite often as well. His walls were decorated with quotes from different African American figures, specifically highlighting many pieces from the late great, Bob Marley. His kitchen was equipped with all black appliances, although the large space was barley utilized, causing the area to appear brand new.

He was in dire need of an alcoholic beverage, something to keep him focused especially after ending the phone call with his sister. He couldn't believe the news Essence had called him with, and he wanted answers right then and there. Reggie had witnessed many senseless incidents between Jade and King, but he never thought his boy would take things this far and put ole girl in the hospital. Reggie called all of King's lines only to be graced by his disdainful voicemail every single time. The unanswered calls caused him to reach out to King's right hand man, Trick, but his line was dry as a whistle as well.

Feeling a bit defeated, Reggie removed his feet from the ottoman and stood to stretch his stiff body, which hadn't been moved since he returned home from New York a few hours ago. His body was drained after enduring the flight home, especially after having to conduct the conference all alone, which he now realized was a reckless decision he made. Although he felt his decision was foolish, his pride just wouldn't allow him to face Patience after the stunt she pulled at the bar.

After what seemed like a long twenty minutes of stretching, Reggie went to his mini bar which was connected to his kitchen and poured himself a shot of Lagavulin, a whiskey that you definitely couldn't find at your local bar or liquor store. He lived for collecting items, liquor being one of the many items on the list, and his mini bar proved to be worth a hundred thousand in itself. He picked up his glass from the counter and took the contents straight to the head, which caused his face to squint a little due to the strong taste. He shook his head to familiarize his body with the feeling before pouring a second glass and repeating the process. The drinks gave him just the feeling he needed, but caused him to become a little warm, so he headed into his large bedroom to open the balcony doors.

He stepped outside and looked into the stunning night's sky, admiring his beautiful city from twelve levels in the air. The ringing of his phone broke his concentration, as he ran into the house almost falling trying to answer before the caller hung up. He was hoping that King was on the line, calling back to clear up the misunderstanding, but he was wrongly mistaken as he seen "Ziva" flash across the screen. He hit the ignore button and returned to his room flopping sluggishly on his King sized bed.

He laid back and enjoyed the cool breeze that flowed into his room from the open balcony doors, while pressing the call button on King's number for the hundredth time; with no luck at all. The alcohol and the wind caused his eyes to flutter repeatedly until there was no more fight left in him. Reggie fell into a deep night's rest as his ringing phone fell to the floor with the same name continuing to flash on the screen.

Reggie spent the next few days trying to track down his childhood friend, while praying that he didn't have any involvement in Jade's shooting.

Reggie knew that he and King ventured separate paths in life, and to be honest he knew that their friendship held very little in common now which caused things to become different between the two.

Despite the changes in their friendship, Reggie still felt that he knew King. He couldn't imagine King taking the sucker route out and at the same time playing himself off the streets all over some pussy. He knew King's history of being arrogant and disrespectful towards women; with the daily mental abuse he inflicted upon them all, but he couldn't imagine King harming any of them, especially not Jade.

King's disappearing act is making him look guilty as hell. If the nigga is innocent, why is he hiding? Reggie silently thought as he grabbed his keys and headed out of the door, not being able to sit still without answers any longer.

Reggie rode to all of their old anonymous spots that they utilized back when Reggie was deep in the streets. No one had seen him around, and that was strange as hell because King checked up on things in the hood daily to ensure proper operations. Reggie noticed unmarked cruisers on every corner he visited, which fed his curiosity on King's connection. He felt that going to the clubs would be absurd due to the fact that APD was on his trail; he figured that King had enough sense to steer clear of his businesses.

The entire situation was wild to him and his standpoint on the whole issue was neutral due to the different relationships he had with them both. He hated the idea of getting involved in other people's private matters; he had seen firsthand of how detrimental that could be in the long run. He was done searching for King, and he was officially done preaching to Jade about loving herself first. He felt that the only help he could give them would be prayer, in hopes of them both waking up to reality.

Reggie took one last look at himself in the mirror while spraying on his Hugo Boss cologne, wanting to smell extra edible since Patience would be at the office for the first day of internship. He smiled at his reflection, while admiring his black sleeved, gray chested Jil Sander blazer, which gave him a very rugged businesslike appeal.

His mind was running a thousand miles per minute as a tingling sensation took over his body at the anticipation of actually seeing Patience again. The feeling was unfamiliar, but he enjoyed the moment, allowing his defenses to rest a little. He was slowly getting over how Patience had played him back in New York. At the same time, he slowly accepted the fact that he was indeed intrigued by the young lady. Reggie thought that she was truly something special if she made him feel like this. She invaded his thoughts a little too much, especially after only having one initial interaction with her. The feelings he was feeling were beyond his control and there was nothing he could do about it.

Control was his number one rule, but he was losing every piece of control left in his body from the mere thought of someone he barely knew. Patience had his mind all screwed up to the point he was willing to break rule number two and mix business with pleasure if she wanted to take it there with him.

How could a woman I barely know have me tripping like this? What's really good with this shit? Reggie thought as he clicked the keypad to unlock the garage and jumped into his silver and black Maserati truck.

Reggie had finally decided that he was going to ask Patience out on a date after assigning her to an office and presenting the caseloads to her. He wasn't expecting for it to be anything major; he just needed to see if she held the least bit of interest in him as he did her. He hadn't asked a woman out in so long that considering it felt quite awkward, but there was no turning back now.

Reggie was used to women throwing themselves at him, which was something that he'd grown to hate over the years. He felt that the man should always be the aggressor and never the woman. He smiled at himself, swinging his dreads backwards and tying them high above his head. He looked at his mocha colored skin and the fullness of his face in the mirror and for the first time ever questioned his features.

Patience really had him going in circles. Her detached personality caused him to feel a bit insecure. Reggie had always been sure of himself, but her lack of interest caused every alarm to go off in his analytical head. He concluded that her blasé demeanor was what drew him to her. It sparked an interest like none ever before while she held no interest whatsoever towards him.

Reggie slowly pulled his car from the garage. As he approached the exit to turn onto Seventeenth Street, a yellow Dodge Magnum with black stripes parked at the curb prevented him from leaving the building. Out of reflex, Reggie reached for his double action old school that he had concealed in a hidden compartment made into the 15" display screen on the dash. He cocked it and paid very close attention to his surroundings, not liking the scene unfolding right in front of him. Reggie edged closer to the car, almost bumping it getting prepared to bust first and ask questions later.

The view in his peripheral caused him to slowly drop the gun and place the truck in park. Patience sexily strutted out of the building looking as beautiful as ever. Her curly hair was all over the place and her natural features were so dynamic they could've been featured on the cover of a magazine. Reggie could smell her sweet scent from his truck and they were almost twenty feet away from each other. The vibrant business dress she wore hugged every curve on her body causing her booty to jiggle lightly. Her plump lips remained constant and her facial expression was neutral which indicated that she showed no excitement about reuniting with the driver.

The driver's door opened and out came Dude, which caused Reggie to frown and nervously bite his bottom lip. Dude beamed a nervous boyish grin as he followed behind Patience to open the passenger door for her. Her body smoothly slid into the black leather interior of the car and she disappeared right before his eyes.

Reggie was mesmerized by her; in fact, he was too stunned to even think logically during that moment. He felt so many mixed emotions, not understanding where any of the feelings were coming from. He was curious and wanted to know how long she had been this close to him without him even knowing it. His mind was in overdrive now and he desperately wanted to know if she was really seeing Dude's lame ass. He dreaded the thought of it, but he needed to know exactly how serious they were.

Reggie knew that Patience was scheduled to come into the clinic that morning for her first official day of internship, so he pulled off right behind them in hopes of making it there before they did. He turned up his audio and allowed Rocko's *You and I* to blast through the speakers. The lyrics caused him to think of Patience. He quickly changed the song and sped through downtown Atlanta to the clinic.

Reggie arrived to the clinic in twenty minutes flat and proceeded to his office to make a few important phone calls. After finishing up his calls, he heard a soft knock at his door, which he figured to be Stacy so he buzzed her in. To his surprise, Patience stood before him staring him down with a slight twinge in her eyes. Reggie was distracted, but his street nature allowed him to appear otherwise as he instructed Patience to have a seat on the sectional closest to his large desk.

"Good Morning!" Reggie spoke first to clear the thin air between them.

Patience looked up at Reggie and smiled; something he rarely saw her do during their time in New York.

"How rude of me to enter without speaking. Good morning, Mr. Dupree. So much on my mind these days, I guessed I blanked out a little."

Reggie soaked in her statement, trying to figure out if he should use this as the opportunity to pop the big question to her.

"Is everything good, Patience? Do you want to talk about it later over dinner?"

The questions of concern just poured from his mouth without him even realizing it. One part of him was happy that it was over with, but the other part of him was reluctant to hear her answer.

Patience smile disappeared and a blank expression appeared on her face. Reggie couldn't read it at all and that was strange because he was in the line of business of reading people's inner thoughts. He felt crushed and he regretted his actions before she even spoke.

"No disrespect, Mr. Dupree, but I'm here to complete my internship and gain hours towards graduation. I expect nothing neither more nor less to occur while I'm working to do so. I'm not the average female that you're used to dealing with, and I would appreciate it if you respected that fact."

Reggie initial response was the biting of his lip. They both knew that he was becoming nervous; she had seen him do that in her presence quite a few times. Reggie stood from his desk and walked over to Patience. They were both staring at each other and nether was willing to back down.

Patience stood up to gain leverage; she never preferred looking up to anyone. Once to her feet, she realized that she had no other choice except to look up because Reggie's six-foot frame towered over her like a giant.

Reggie reached for her hand and forced a shake of agreement, which caused Patience to look at him as if he were crazy. Reggie noticed her facial expression. Before she could speak, he started.

"Look, I want to apologize about my reaction back in New York. I felt you were in danger and I wanted to rectify the situation before it got out of hand. Yea, I was surprised to see your reaction, especially when you left with him, but I guess I don't know everything. Matter of fact I don't know much about you at all. I want to make your internship here as comfortable as possible, and I never want you to mistake my manners as a lack of respect for you. I want us to start off fresh and make today a new beginning for us both with Dupree Youth Behavioral."

Reggie finally let Patience regain custody of her hand and tilted his head to the side.

"Do you accept my apology?"

Patience was literally melting on the inside and she couldn't believe it. She wanted so badly to smile as she watched him intelligently redeem himself, but she couldn't allow any sign to be shown to him.

"Yes, Mr. Dupree, I do," was her simple reply.

The rest of the day seemed to fly by as Reggie showed Patience all of the ins and outs of the business. He assigned her to an office near his, and gave Patience her very first caseload of twenty youths. He trained her on everything from accessing the clinics software, making the weekly call checks to the other clinics, signing in on the state's database, to the proper communications and functions of other contracted state programs.

When lunchtime came around Stacy had ordered Jason's Deli for the staff, which gave Reggie and Patience a minute to wind down. Patience and Reggie ate their sandwiches in his office while continuing the extensive training session. The air between them was becoming very comfortable, even to the point where they both would catch themselves laughing during awkward moments.

"You chew like a cow Mr. Dupree, stop it!" Patience laughed as she wiped the remains of mayo from her mouth and pressed her little finger into Reggie's chest.

Reggie chuckled and placed his hands up in the air as in a defeating manner, "Excuse my manners, I was hungry, and not eating breakfast had me all into that sandwich. By the way call me Reggie; you make me feel like an old man with the Mr. Dupree salutation."

Patience shook her head signaling that she was okay with calling him on a first name basis. She was becoming nervous again and it was becoming hard for her to hide the attraction so she stood to walk into her office that was connected to Reggie's office by a small wooden door. Before entering, she looked back and caught Reggie staring intensely at her. Her words became jumbled, but the little pride left in her allowed her to speak.

"I'm going to finish up my review on the last three cases, and I'll come back with a run down when done."

Reggie turned his head to his computer screen after being caught staring.

"That's cool. After the run down, I'll have something for you to take back to the college with you tomorrow. I'm going to prepare and approve a special conditions letter for you. The letter will basically state that since you're on the last year of your Master's degree, you can finish up your internship here along with out of class on the job training."

Patience stepped back into his side of the office and looked at him with yet another blank expression on her face, "What are you saying?"

Reggie turned his head from the computer and looked right into her beautiful eyes, "I'm saying that I want to hire you directly on here at Dupree Youth Behavioral to finish your educational efforts allowing you to gain full paid experience, only leaving your capstone final paper for your professor."

Patience approached him and her defensive side came into full effect.

"Look Reggie, I don't need handouts. I'm a big girl and can take care of myself just fine. I see that we both have very big egos, and just from our few interactions, I can see that it's a challenge for us to even be in each other's presence. If you are doing this with an ulterior motive, please know that it is not needed. I can only accept things that I deserved fully on my own."

Reggie agreed with Patience completely; he operated the exact same way. He couldn't honestly say that he extended the offer just because of her great work on her first day; he definitely extended the offer just to be near her. He felt a connection with her and he wanted more of her. Hearing her thoughts softened him, but his own selfish needs took over as he did what he felt was best.

"Patience calm down, I'm extending this offer to you because I see the potential that you have. I can honestly feel your drive and love for the youth, and it's only your first day interning here. Your dedication is fully here already; look at you, you're almost done completing reviews that would have taken others weeks to do. I know how hard it is juggling work, internship, and college and I just want to help make things easier for you. I'm going forward with extending this offer, which will consist of a starting salary of eight thousand a month, on the job training towards your degree, working/interning here three days a week. You have a month to accept before the offer is null and void, so take your time and really consider this."

Patience stared Reggie up and down in total disbelief at his offer, lost in her thoughts. *What did I possibly do to deserve this? What's up with this man? Ok, I must stop over thinking things and*

*accept the damn offer. This is my chance to cut ties
with the club scene and focus solely on my career. I
won't let my blessings pass me by.*

Patience's inner excitement allowed her body
to react in such a way that was new to her. The
pride and toughness Patience normally possessed
disappeared for a moment; allowing her to soften up
a tad bit, something that seemed to happen quite
often when in Reggie's presence. She didn't like the
unfamiliar feeling because it made her feel
powerless, but she would deal with it for now.

She rushed to Reggie and hugged him tightly
almost knocking him from his reclining chair.

"Thank you so much for this opportunity.
Although I don't know or understand your
reasoning for doing this, I promise that you won't
be disappointed."

Reggie was shocked by Patience's drastic
change of reaction and braced himself for his
response. Patience wild hair was surrounding his
face, and her sweet scent caused chills to form up
and down his spine. She held both of her arms

around his neck and placed both of his arms around her waist. He wanted that moment to last forever but he quickly removed his arms not wanting her to feel uncomfortable. Seconds passed and Patience still held the tight embrace around Reggie's neck; he simply enjoyed the moment without uttering a sound.

After Patience came back into his office with the rundown of the cases, he went over everything with her about the offer. His day was a long one, but indeed a great one so Reggie decided to lock up the office, allowing all of the employees to leave an hour early for the day. They both laughed and had light conversation as Reggie showed Patience how to do a quick check of the building before leaving.

As he turned off all of the office lights preparing to leave, they both were distracted from the awkward silence by loud music blasting from outside of the building. They both proceeded to the front door and the great feeling Reggie once felt vanished after noticing Dude's yellow Magnum parked out front.

Reggie held the door open for Patience to exit and walked her to the car while eyeing down Dude who nervously sat in the driver's seat looking away from his evil glare before speaking.

"Next time, keep the music to a minimum; this is a place of business."

When they pulled off his mood was all fucked up again. His emotions were getting the best of him and he had to do something to put a stop to it all. He felt defeated and he was angry with himself for being a chump for a chick he knew nothing about. His ego was bruised and he needed something that would fix it immediately. As he walked to the truck, he pulled his iPhone from his pants pocket and scrolled through the missed calls from Ziva the night before. His phone blinked and a message boxed popped up reminding him that he had ten percent remaining on his battery, but he ignored it and pressed call on Ziva's name.

She answered on the second ring and before she could even say hello, Reggie's baritone voice blared through her speaker, "Come to the office NOW!"

Ziva cleared her throat and asked, "Is everything ok, Reggie? You don't sound like yourself?"

Reggie cut her off again. "Just do as I say," he demanded. "Meet me in the parking lot in twenty."

Those twenty minutes felt like seconds as Ziva followed Reggie's command and arrived in less than ten minutes. Ziva was one of the few chicks that he kept on standby but held the least bit of interest in her. She was a beauty indeed, but was too needy and gullible for his likings.

She arrived dressed in a little red dress and red pumps that Reggie was prepared to tear right off her body. As she approached the truck, Reggie pulled her in and sat her right on top of his lap. Ziva tried to speak but Reggie placed one finger on her lips and she knew instantly what that meant. He didn't do any speaking as his hands ripped her dress from her body. He performed roughly and handled her like a tramp off the streets, but she didn't protest or stop him. They both drifted off into a passion of lust without a care in the world, not even noticing the car that was slowly approaching them.

CHAPTER 11

I am hard pressed between the two.
My desire is to depart and be with Christ, for
that is far better. But to remain in the flesh is
more necessary on your account. Philippians
1:23-24

JADE

Jade reached her hands out towards her mother
who floated angelically in the air surrounding her.
She wanted so badly to touch her as she extended
her arms even further, trying her best, but still not
being able to feel her. Jade was finally at peace
now. Seeing her mother for the first time in years
assured her that everything was going to be just
fine. She stared intensely at her mother, deciding to
give up on reaching for her at that moment.

She noticed her mother's dark chocolate skin
that hauntingly glowed, sending a sense of calmness

through her entire body. Her mother reached out to her and placed her hands on top of hers while chanting an unfamiliar chant. Jade smiled at her mother, admiring her striking beauty, coming to the realization that she was really reunited with her queen. Jade removed her hands from her mother's grip craving to hug her, yet as she reached out her hands, she felt nothing but thin air. Jade felt defeated, but the beautiful scenery surrounding her caused her to remain composed.

Jade's lifeless body rested as she floated deeper into the snow white clouds. Her mother slowly drifted backwards, smiling and waving while heading towards a winding stairway. Jade tried to speak but she couldn't. She tried to follow her mom, but she was stuck. She tried to cry, but no emotions were present. Then there it was, something she thought she would never hear again came flowing out with so much love. The beautiful sound gave her a feeling that she never felt before, a feeling that caused her to become content.

"My sweet dearest princess; the love of my life then and now. Do not fight to get where I am just yet. Your time will soon come to pass."

With her emotions being held captive by a force alien to her, she couldn't muster a word. Jade simply watched her beautiful mother, a reflection of herself ascend into the heavens of the earth.

****

The serene peace that once covered her body was now gone, as pain riddled throughout her body and the taste of blood filled her lungs. She coughed uncontrollably as she began to shake, feeling her body going into convulsions. She faintly heard the commotion surrounding her. Heat flashed on the inside of her body, and the feeling of death overtook her as she found it hard to breath. With all of the machinery hooked up to her body, she still felt lifeless as images of her dad appeared before her causing her to drift off into another place.

ACKNOWLEDGEMENTS

I would like to start by saying thank you to ALL of my readers for taking the time out of your busy schedules to purchase and read my very first novel, "Secrets In The A". Words can't express how I appreciate all of the love that was shown through the many reviews, emails, and social network shutouts. I received all of the support in the world from you guys and for that I will forever be grateful! I LOVE my reader's for simply giving me a chance and motivating me to continue on this journey of revealing the words from my soul. I pray that you all are BLESSED beyond measures, and I hope that you all enjoy my second novel, which I present to you now!

Next, I would like to recognize my family whom I love with everything in me. To my mother, Barbara Smith, your words of wisdom and motivation are the essential pieces to my puzzle. You are the epitome of a beautiful queen, my beautiful queen, a woman of respect, love, and loyalty. BTW, I'm so happy that this book will be in print so that you can read it without getting on my nerves about all of the electronic gadgets… (lol).

To my father James Stanley, I am truly grateful to have you in my life. You may didn't always do what I wanted you to do, but you've always done all that you could to ensure that I was happy. They say there's nothing like a father's love and I must agree with that saying 1000%.

To my sister Coretta Smith-Hixon, I would like to thank you for always being that positive role model in my life. I remember back when I was in elementary school and the teachers would ask, "Who is your role model?" All of my classmates would respond by naming someone rich/famous and it's crazy because I was the only odd ball. My answer was, "My big sister Coretta". You probably would have never known this until now, but yep you were and still are my role model. The excitement on your face after reading my first novel will forever remain etched in my heart. You wanted to know what would happen next one minute and then the next minute you wanted me to stop telling you. I appreciate your support and I want you to know that you shock me daily with your beauty and your brains, providing me with a love that is so irreplaceable.

To my cousin, my love, my FAV Briunca Hart, I am so appreciative of the relationship that we have built throughout the years. We went from never seeing each other growing up, to seeing each other occasionally during holidays and family events, to not wanting to be away from one another now. God brought us closer for a reason and as long as I'm living I want us to always maintain our bond. You were the very first person to read "Secrets In The A", and the first to read "To Love Honor And Betray". Your support is amazing, and a blessing to have. I have family members & friends who didn't support me, but the simple fact that you did means so much to me.

To my other cousins, Shanteria Young, Domeci Corbin, Shaqueta Corbin, Konstanza Latimer,

Demetrius Turner, Derius Turner, Zion Hart &
Myka Delancy, Mechael Coffield ,Syera Smith,
Keyoka Smith, Tyon Smith, Carolyn Smith, Tracy
Smith, Marsha Hart, Coretta Hart… And the many
others that I didn't name, I just want you to know
that I LOVE YOU ALL!!!!

To my friends, I just want to say that you guys
give me so many of my great ideas. Sometimes I
think to myself, "What would I do without y'all??"
To Princess Henderson, my fatty cakes, I love you
and I admire your strength and independence. Our
friendship started in 7th grade at Young Middle
School and we still remain the best of friends. Make
sure you go get both copies so that you can see this
acknowledgement; you know how you go out to
purchase the new burgers that come out lol.

To Desiree Johnson, my white girl, my sweetie,
Tiger's "Polo Girl", I just want you to know that
your friendship is irreplaceable. Your heart is so big
and your actions are so selfless, I couldn't ask for a
better friend better yet a better little sister. You and

Serenity Cobb are my FAMILY and I love you two like you could never imagine. I know Tiger is smiling down & I know that he is enjoying his 1st in memory of page in this novel. Coolie, Aunt Mary, Aunt Betty, Jessi, Juicy… "HEY Yall, Love you all as well)

To Jaz'min Johnson, my "Mary Alice Sue, I love you and the girls (Nevaeh Hines, Tamia Hines, & Ms. Gale Harvey) so much. The love that the girls have for me is astonishing; they surely can feel the love that I show them is genuine. You are a woman of GOD that I'm waiting to see transform just into the person you are destined to be. In the middle of me writing this you called & you gave me words of motivation just as I was second guessing myself. You told me to never give up because I'm going to make a difference in kids' lives. You told me that this is only the beginning. Well, I just want you to know that God have great things in store for you. I want you to go & get your blessings baby without any distractions. You are destined to be something very special, I see in you something GREAT!!!

To Author Lataryn Rainey-Perry, HELLO lady!!! It was a pleasure meeting you through the art of our works this year. Starting off as new authors we both did the thing and I am very proud of you. We're in two different states, yet we still supported each other majorly. We both have great ideas and plans ahead of us & I'm ready for it all.

To Author "Tajana Sutton", my very first publisher, I would like to thank you for having my back and allowing me to share my gift with the world through your publishing company. It was an honor working with you, and I pray that we can stay in touch for future projects!

To my new publisher, Sevyn McCray… I thank you for allowing me to travel on this new path with you. Being one of the first authors of your publishing company, "Peach Dollhouse", is truly a blessing. You are a very talented lady, with much class and attitude. You are a great author, a great mentor, and a very wise woman. You gave me great advice and ideas that pushed me to write more and want more. I pray that this partnership grows into something truly great. I'm so ready to write more and challenge myself with great things. ATLANTA has bred some very talented ladies and I'm ready to take our talent/gift to higher levels.

To Cookie, "Divalicious Salon", thanks for the love and the support. I will finally be hosting my first book signing in your beautiful salon!! Henry, I'm glad you love the shop and I'm proud of your accomplishments!

To my Department of Juvenile Justice family (My fellow Probation/Parolee Officers), I would like to give you all a shout out for being genuinely great people and helping me adapt to my new position.. (Bush "Comedian", Hicks-King "Best Manager EVER", Fern Clarke "We Miss YOU", Farley "My training buddy", Whitby "Training buddy", Jordan "Crazy", McCollough "Respectful", Lewis "Laid Back", Gaines "Clever", Blakely "Future-Lawyer", Grigsby "Leader", Hampton "Cool Dude", Brown "Serious Natured", Rankins "Team Player", McCord "Quiet", Gordan "Congrats New Mommy", Ms.Gilchrist & Ms. Merenu "Best PA's EVER"!!!

To all of my other friends and family, I love you guys & I have not forgotten about all that you've done to assist me on my journey. Thank You, Thank you, Thank you for EVERYTHING!!!

To my new readers, I would like to thank you for purchasing "To Love Honor And Betray". I pray that this book touches your heart and soul and leave you craving for more. Enjoy your read and be sure to leave an honest review on Amazon & Barnes & Noble. Also, make sure that you follow my social network pages listed below. PEACE & LOVE TO ALL!!!

ABOUT
THE
AUTHOR

Crystal Smith is a 25 year old NEW African American Author that has loved the art of literature ever since she could remember. Growing up she spent majority of her time writing short stories, poems, and music. She completed her first novel "Secrets in the A", at age 19 after graduating from Benjamin E Mays High School in Atlanta Georgia (2006). She later went on to attend Bauder College majoring in Criminal Justice while leaving her writing dreams behind for a short time.

After years of completing amazing college papers, she decided to send her works to different publishing companies. In 2013 she was recognized by Ruby Love Publications and became one of the new authors of the publishing company, with her novel "Secrets In The A" being released on Friday April5, 2013. After releasing her first novel Crystal begin working on new projects and was discovered by Peach Doll House Publications, becoming one of the first authors to be signed, with her novel "To Love Honor & Betray."

Crystal currently resides in Atlanta, Georgia, employed as a Juvenile Probation/Parole Officer for the State of Georgia. She is currently working on other great projects, so keep your eyes open readers and be on the lookout for the name CRYSTAL SMITH. There's plenty more coming to a bookstore near YOU!!!

DEDICATION

Father God just as I dedicated my life to you, just as I dedicated my first novel to you, it wouldn't be right if I didn't dedicate this novel to its rightful owner. I simply thank you for allowing me to watch my dreams come alive; dreams that I never thought would come true. You deserve the honor and praise for this spectacular piece of work, and to you the honor and praise shall go!

Delight yourself in the lord, and he will give you the desires of your heart. –Psalms37:4

In Loving Memory

Of

Arkenius Cobb "Tyga"

March 1989 – September 2011

Although you are absent from the body, your memories and the many thoughts of you are present here in our hearts. Although your smile is gone away, God somehow made it possible for us to see it yet another day. The angel you left behind bears your smile and your heart, God knew what he was doing way from the very start. I wish that you could be here to see her grow and learn, she's been everyone's pride and joy, giving us the strength we need to go on. When I say "Go On", I don't mean forget that you were here. That's something that we could never forget as long as we're left here. Although you are loved and missed very dearly, that could never bring you back. I pray we've all learned a lesson from you and wear it as a weapon on our backs. – Crystal Smith

We understand death for the first time when he puts his hand upon one whom we love. ~**Madame de Stael**

"They that love beyond the world cannot be separated by it. Death cannot kill what never dies." ~ **Williams Penn**

CONTACT INFORMATION

CONNECT WITH CRYSTAL SMITH!

IG: author_CrystalSmith

Twitter: @iWriteBooksCJS (Author Crystal Smith)

Facebook: Author Crystal Smith

COPYRIGHT INFORMATION

To Love. Honor, and Betray

Copyright 2013 by Crystal Smith
Published by Peach Dollhouse Publications
Cover Art by Brittani Williams
All rights reserved

This book is a work of fiction. Names, characters, places, and incidents either are the product of the author's imagination or are used fictitiously and are not to be construed as real. Any resemblance to actual persons, living or dead, business establishments, events, or locales or, is entirely coincidental.

No part of this book may be used or reproduced in any manner without the permission of the publisher except in the case of using brief quotes for review or articles pertaining to this work. For information, contact

Peach Dollhouse Publications

P. O. Box 116

Atlanta, Georgia 30272-0116.

Table of Contents

Proof

24424333R00126

Made in the USA
Charleston, SC
22 November 2013